"A man knows when his territory is shaky."

Leslie shouted back over the roar of the traffic, "My relationship with Stephen is not shaky!"

Their jeep stopped for a red light. Leaning toward her, he said, his voice intimate, "I've kissed you, remember? A woman who's committed to a man doesn't respond like that in someone else's arms—"

"The light's green," Leslie interrupted urgently.

But as the jeep began moving, he continued, "And I'll tell you another thing, Les, just so things are fair. I'm not going to let up. Old Stevie's got a fight on his hands."

Although his arrogance annoyed her, Leslie couldn't stop the strange thrill coursing through her at his warning. Just the same, she had no intention of getting involved with this man who had turned her life upside down.

WELCOME
TO THE WONDERFUL WORLD
OF *Harlequin Romances*

Interesting, informative and entertaining,
each Harlequin Romance portrays an appealing
and original love story. With a varied array
of settings, we may lure you on an African safari,
to a quaint Welsh village, or an exotic Riviera
location—anywhere and everywhere that adventurous
men and women fall in love.

As publishers of Harlequin Romances, we're
extremely proud of our books. Since 1949,
Harlequin Enterprises has built its publishing
reputation on the solid base of quality and
originality. Our stories are the most popular
paperback romances sold in North America; every
month, six new titles are released and sold at
nearly every book-selling store in Canada and the
United States.

For a list of all titles currently available,
send your name and address to:

HARLEQUIN READER SERVICE,
(In the U.S.) P.O. Box 52040, Phoenix, AZ 85072-2040
(In Canada) P.O. Box 2800, Postal Station A
5170 Yonge Street, Willowdale, Ont. M2N 6J3

We sincerely hope you enjoy reading
this Harlequin Romance.

Yours truly,

THE PUBLISHERS
Harlequin Romances

Quiet Lightning

Tracy Hughes

Harlequin Books

TORONTO • NEW YORK • LONDON
AMSTERDAM • PARIS • SYDNEY • HAMBURG
STOCKHOLM • ATHENS • TOKYO • MILAN

ISBN 0-373-02744-3

Harlequin Romance first edition February 1986

CHAPTER ONE

"DO SOCIETY A FAVOR and stick your head in the oven," the deep voice said from the speaker above Leslie Torrence's head. "Ignorant pervert." *Click.* "This is Nick Nemoy, go ahead."

Leslie's jaws ached, but she continued to grind her molars together with unceasing pressure. Her fingernails bit into her palms, and her knuckles turned white. She listened in the lobby of the New Orleans radio station as another courageous listener dared to state an opinion.

"Is it just me or is everybody out there dense?" the host asked. "I can't believe you'd actually defend the Republican party."

"I'm not defending them," the caller said. "I happen to be a Democrat."

"Then that explains your naive mentality," Nick snapped in his clipped, condescending voice. *Click.* "Hello, you're on the air. Make it quick."

Leslie leaned on the edge of the receptionist's vacant desk and clutched her purse against her stomach. What would she say to the man who had done so much damage to her parents' marriage? Nothing came to mind, but she trusted her instincts to take over when she came face-to-face with the notorious Nick Nemoy. By now her mother was on a plane halfway to San Juan, about to take the cruise she and Leslie's father had planned for years. But her father was at home, working on some cabinets he insisted on building for an old favorite customer whose home had been destroyed in a fire. A workaholic, her mother had called him. Even in retirement, he wouldn't slow down. Leslie breathed a ragged sigh. They could have compromised, she thought, if her mother had not called Nick Nemoy for on-the-air advice. "Divorce the schmuck," Nick had said in his crisp thoughtless way. And the next morning, her mother had filed for a legal separation and packed to take the cruise her father refused.

She glanced at her watch and saw that it was ten o'clock. Time for his show to go off the air. Any minute now a fat, obnoxious little man with the stubble of a cigar between his teeth and bloodshot eyes would burst through that door and spot her. She couldn't wait to tell him what she thought of him. *Just don't let your temper get the best of you,* she reminded herself. *He's a master at humiliating people and getting them flustered.*

She took a deep breath as Nemoy finished with his last caller, a woman complaining about a low-income apartment complex being constructed in her middle-class neighborhood. "Can't have all the riffraff playing with your kids, can we?" Nick said. "How dare they expect to live where they choose?"

"It's not that," the woman argued. "It's the value of my property I'm worried about."

"Afraid your geraniums will get stepped on as the lower classes overrun the area?"

"That's not what—"

"Sorry, lady. If you want an argument, go to your husband. Our time's up." *Click.* "And now that I've got all those sick little minds out there juiced up, it's time to go. Just hold that ingenious thought until tomorrow night. This is Nick Nemoy, signing off."

His theme music faded out and a popular record began playing. *Any minute now,* Leslie thought. She stood up and paced the lobby, looking at the doorway for some sign of life. She could hear an exchange of muffled voices down the hall, then a quick rustle of pant legs coming closer. Stepping toward the door, she stood with her feet a little apart, arms folded across her chest with guarded determination. She raised her chin and wished she were taller. Five foot six wasn't bad, but she'd like to be bigger, more intimidating, to the likes of Nick Nemoy. Her dark hair was swept back from her face and lifted off her neck in a loose French twist, and she hoped it looked severe enough to counteract her innocent face and round green eyes. Straightening her blazer, she moved a little nearer to the door. Footsteps echoed hers, and she braced herself for the face-to-face encounter with Nick Nemoy.

The man who walked through the door was not the one she expected. Standing just over six feet, he was young—no older than thirty-five, she guessed—and had a full head of blond hair and a lifeguard's tan. His dark-brown, almost black eyes registered surprise at her presence, but the surprise soon faded and a pleasant smile lit them. "Hello, ma'am. May I help you?" he asked with the slightest hint of a southern drawl.

She relaxed, deciding to save her frost for the real thing. "I'm Leslie Torrence. Who are you?"

He reached for her hand and shook it warmly, his eyes never leaving hers. "I'm Scott Jenkins. Nice meeting you." He dropped her hand and, tilting his head, let his eyes take in her body. Leslie pulled her blazer closed, suddenly wishing she'd worn a blouse that didn't define her breasts so clearly, and perhaps a looser skirt than the one that hugged her hips and emphasized the curves of her derriere. "So, Leslie Torrence," he said, his eyes rising back to hers, "what in the world brings you here?"

"Nick Nemoy," she said, feeling heat rising in her cheeks. "I'd like to speak to him. Would you please tell him I'm here?"

"Does he know you?" the man asked, his smile fading. His eyes narrowed, wrinkling the little laugh lines beside them.

Leslie raised her chin again. "No, Mr. Nemoy has not had the pleasure."

A slow grin spread across his face, and a dimple appeared on one cheek. "And what is it you'd like to see him about?"

Leslie shifted her purse from one shoulder to the other. "I'd like to speak to him about some of the things he's been saying on this show."

"Are you from the FCC?" he asked, referring to the Federal Communications Commission, a government regulatory agency. A furrow formed between his brows, which were darker than his hair.

"No," she said. "I'm here as a concerned citizen who feels he's gone a little too far on more than one occasion."

"I see," Scott said, leaning a shoulder on the jamb of the doorway. "So you came to set him straight?"

"Precisely. Now please go tell him I'm here."

Scott shrugged. "Can't. He's already left. He always leaves through the other exit in case 'concerned citizens' like you are waiting for him." He lifted his hand and examined a fingernail, then buffed it on his shirt. "Old Nick—he's not very popular, you know."

"Yes, I can imagine," she said, looking at her feet, trying to decide what to do next. She glanced back up at the man who had stepped closer to her, hands in pockets. "Do you work for him?"

"Sure do," he drawled. A stray strand of hair had fallen over one eye and was caught between his lashes. "I'm an engineer of sorts."

"How can you stand it?" She felt her face flush with renewed anger and stepped toward him. "He hurts people. The man is crazy and he actually has his own show. He gives people advice, and some of those listeners follow it."

Scott threw his head back and laughed. "No ma'am. I doubt anyone really follows it."

"I'm telling you they do. There are some people out there who simply want a little guidance. They're willing to do anything they're told by someone on the radio, simply because they believe he wouldn't be there if he didn't know what he was doing."

Scott went to the coatrack and pulled down a gray windbreaker. "Well, I guess you do have a bone to pick with him, then. I'll tell you what. Why don't I buy you a cup of coffee and we can talk about this? If I think it's something that needs to come to Nick's attention, I'll see that you get an appointment with him. How's that sound?" He hooked the coat with a finger and flung it over his shoulder.

Leslie studied the man, wondering if everyone in association with Nick Nemoy was a tiny bit demented. Well, it wasn't as if she couldn't take care of herself, she thought. She knew how to handle a lech, if she needed to.

As if reading her thoughts, Scott grinned and raised his eyebrows. "Come on. I'm a nice guy. Look at me."

She did, knowing that what she saw was unusually appealing, knowing that he, too, was keenly aware of his attractiveness. "Well, maybe just a cup of coffee."

"And some stimulating conversation," he added with a wink, touching the small of her back and ushering her out of the radio station.

The night air was damp and cool, and Leslie smelled rain. They sky was starless. In the distance, the clouds lit up with a silent flash of lightning. "There's going to be a storm," she said, glancing up at the man beside her.

"Good." He stopped to gaze down at her, took the jacket off his shoulder and folded it over an arm. "This is my car," he said, pointing to a silver Mercedes. "Why don't you ride with me?"

Leslie shook her head. "No. I think I'll just follow you."

Scott grinned and his dimple creased again. "Oh, come on. I swear I'm a nice guy. After you have coffee with me, you just won't believe what a great guy I am."

Leslie tried to fight the smile breaking across her face. "Great guy or not, I don't make a habit of getting stuck in situations I can't control."

"Stuck?" he repeated. "Did you say stuck? I'm hurt." He rested his knuckles on his hips and cocked his head. "The lady doesn't want to get stuck with me."

Leslie pursed her lips to keep from grinning. "I didn't mean it that way. And I don't want to make a production out of a simple cup of coffee."

"Then ride with me," he said quietly, resting a hand on her shoulder. "It's good for my ego to drive up to Morgan's with a beautiful woman. Of course, if you're afraid I won't behave myself..." His eyes made an intimate sweep of her body. "I imagine you've had your share of pawers. But I promise you," he said, sliding his hand across to the back of her neck in a gesture that was both intimate and impersonal, making her unsure whether to ignore it or pull away, "I don't take anything that isn't offered. And as far as I can tell, you haven't made any offers yet."

"Yet?" she asked, looking directly into his eyes. She could feel his breath, fresh and clean, on her face. He had been chewing a mint, she decided. "How do you know there's going to be an offer?"

Scott smiled and bit his lip. "Just give me a little time," he said.

Leslie stepped out of his grasp and crossed her arms, but the hint of a grin still sparkled in her eyes. "I'll ride with you, if we're only going as far as Morgan's," she said, opening her purse and pulling out her keys. She held them up and revealed a small can in a leather case attached to the key chain. "Don't be offended if I keep my mace in my hand the whole time. I've found it comes in handy once in a while."

Scott shook his head and laughed. "It's a deal. Just don't keep it aimed at me, okay? It'll affect my driving."

Leslie smiled as he helped her into the car, and she relaxed as he pulled out of the parking lot.

"Do you know Nick Nemoy well?" she asked.

"As well as anybody does, I guess."

"Does he drive a Mercedes, too?" She caught herself on the last word, embarrassed that her curiosity about his financial status had been so obviously expressed.

Scott glanced briefly at her, his face expressionless. "Why do you ask?"

She shrugged and stared at her hands, which were becoming moist in her lap. She wiped them on her skirt, then turned the mace can over in her fingers. "Never mind. That was a stupid question."

"No, it wasn't," he said, smiling slightly. "At least, not if you have a thing for Mercedes. Now if you had some other reason for asking, like a curiosity about how a lowly radio engineer like myself could afford a car like this—"

"No. Of course not," she lied quickly. "It's just that, well, I was surprised, that's all. I mean, I'd expect Nick Nemoy to be rolling in money. He probably gambles and cons people for donations...."

"And takes candy from babies?" His eyes were on the road, but an amused grin worked across his face.

"I wouldn't be surprised," she said with a smile and a lift of her brows, focusing on a spot on the windshield.

Scott reached across the seat and took her hand, as if it was the most natural gesture in the world. "Don't be so hard on Nick. He's just doing his job. And to answer that unasked question of yours, he does make a lot of money. And so do I. We're both valuable commodities."

Leslie pulled her hand out of his, worried he would feel her trembling. "That wasn't what I was getting at," she said. "I wasn't trying to find out how much you make. I just don't know many people with Mercedes." She stopped and sighed. "I also have a habit of putting my foot in my mouth." She leaned her head against the window and tried to concentrate on the neon signs they passed.

"You know, you're downright irresistible when you're embarrassed," he said as he pulled into the parking lot of the popular riverside café.

"I'm not..." she began, then decided to agree so they could get off the subject. "All right, I'm embarrassed."

He touched her chin with his index finger and turned her face to his. She swallowed. "Irresistible," he said, his voice dropping to a whisper. And without warning, he dropped a kiss on the tip of her nose.

Leslie's eyes widened as she jerked back, and Scott threw his hands in front of his face. "I forgot about that can of mace," he said. "Please don't shoot, lady!"

Leslie laughed and shook her head. Well, the evening had not taken the course she had planned, she thought. But it was becoming quite interesting. The man might very well be a lunatic, but he was entertaining.

"Have you been here before?" he asked when he opened her car door. He helped her out, cupping her elbow as they walked.

"Yes. It's one of my favorite places."

"Mine, too," he said. "Funny that I've never seen you here. I'm sure I would have remembered."

"I usually come here for lunch," she explained.

"Then you're missing the best time."

He opened the door and they walked in, and instantly Leslie felt comfortable. A lone guitarist strummed in a corner set apart like a stage, and his soft mellow voice lent an intimate atmosphere to the room. The lighting was different at night, she noted. The room was in a yellow glow from lanterns lighting the tables, instead of the fluorescent ceiling lights used during the day.

Nodding and waving to friends as he passed their tables, Scott led her to a table beside a window looking out over the Mississippi. Each tree on the bank held a lantern that made the water and sleepy hanging moss visible to the diners. The local art and photography displayed on the wall were lit by individual wall lamps.

"You're right," she said after they were seated at right angles to each other. "It is better at night."

He nodded and shifted in his chair to see the musician. "He's good."

Leslie nodded in agreement.

"Do you really feel like coffee?" he asked, leaning toward her on the table to avoid raising his voice. "I kind of feel like a glass of wine."

"Sounds nice," she said, surprised at herself. Never before had she climbed in a car with a total stranger and had wine with him. Oh well, she thought, maybe it was time for a change.

A waitress came to the table and took their order. When the wine arrived, Scott lifted his glass and touched it to Leslie's. "To tonight," he said.

"Tonight?" she asked.

He nodded and sipped, and one side of his mouth crooked in a smile. "For all its surprises and promises."

Reluctantly, Leslie drank, wondering if she had accepted a silent challenge she wasn't prepared for. Across the rim of her glass, she let her eyes answer his smile.

"Green eyes," he said, setting his glass down. "Did I tell you they're my favorite?"

Leslie smiled, unconvinced, and looked out the window. "No, but I'm sure you've told somebody."

He laughed. "I get the feeling you don't find me the most sincere person you've ever known."

Leslie lifted her glass to her lips. "No, but you're smooth. I'll give you that."

"Well, I guess that's something," he said. He set his elbows on the table and rested his chin in his hand, watching her wipe the lip gloss off her glass after she drank. "Now, tell me about yourself," he said. "Beginning with your birth and working right up to the moment you laid eyes on me."

Leslie struggled not to laugh. "Are you always this blunt, or is it just a front for your insecurity?"

"I believe in saying what I think," he admitted, running a finger along the rim of his glass. "Do you consider that a flaw?"

She sipped her wine and let her eyes scan the room to avoid his. "Possibly. I'm not sure."

His eyes narrowed seductively. "But I'm so cute and I'm such a—"

"Great guy," Leslie finished wryly.

"I knew you'd see it soon," he said, leaning back victoriously. He swirled his drink and glanced back at her. "Seriously, though, what do you do for a living? I've already decided you aren't married."

Leslie thought of Stephen Tate, the fourth-year medical student to whom she was unofficially engaged. "And what led you to that conclusion? Lots of people don't wear wedding rings."

"You don't act married," he said. "And by the way, in case you were dying to know, I'm not married, either. Now that that's out of the way, you won't have to feel guilty if you fall in love with me." He paused to wait for her exasperation to color her cheeks. "Now what *do* you do for a living?"

Leslie shook her head and met his eyes. She mustn't encourage this man, she told herself. He was too charming, too attractive. And Stephen, whom she had been seeing for two years, would not be pleased. She cleared her throat and decided to ignore his flirting. "I have a bookkeeping business in my home. I keep the books for several small companies who don't have time to do it themselves, or can't afford to hire someone on a full-time basis. I take care of their payrolls, their taxes, their monthly statements, and whatever else they may need.''

Scott nodded and said, "I'm impressed. The lady is an entrepreneur."

Leslie set down her glass and leaned forward, crossing her arms on the table. "Why do I get the feeling that you've tried to steer me away from the subject of Nick Nemoy?"

Scott raised his eyebrows in innocence. "Me? Have I done that? I didn't mean to. No, if you want to talk about Nick, go ahead."

Leslie's face sobered. No, she didn't really want to spoil this strange unexpected evening by talking about someone she detested. But if she didn't, she'd hate herself the next time she looked at her poor abandoned father. "I really do have to speak to him."

"Are you sure you want to speak to him and not at him? Do you really care what he has to say?"

Leslie straightened. "Yes. I'd love to hear what excuse he has for destroying people's lives."

Scott grinned, but instead of warming her this time, it left her annoyed. "Give me one specific example," he said seriously. "Whose life has been destroyed?"

"My parents," she bit out. "He's ruined their marriage and I don't know if it can be repaired."

Scott arched a brow. "What did he do, sleep with your mother?"

Leslie gasped. "Of course not! My mother is a decent woman."

A grin tugged at Scott's mouth again. "Then what did he do?"

Leslie looked at her drink and forced herself to take a few deep breaths before going on. "They were having a few minor problems. And when my mother called Nick last night and told him about them on the air, he said, and I quote, 'Divorce the schmuck.'"

Scott let out a loud laugh, then covered his mouth. "Did he really say that?"

Leslie did not see the humor. Her eyes glared like laser beams. "Yes, he said that. And this morning my mother filed for a legal separation and took off on a plane to catch a cruise ship in San Juan."

"Good for her!" Scott said with delight.

Leslie's teeth clenched and she clipped her words out through them. "How can you say that?"

Scott leaned forward and touched her hands, but she jerked them back. He spread his palms up. "All I mean is that Nick Nemoy's advice couldn't have caused drastic action like that. If she took those kind of measures, she must have had a good reason. She probably deserves a vacation."

Leslie suddenly felt defenseless. "He called my father a schmuck!"

"Are you an only child?" he asked, as if it had some bearing on the subject.

She looked around the restaurant, reminding herself to keep her voice calm. "Yes. Why?"

"Because you seem so personally affected by your parents' breakup."

"They're my parents. They belong together. They could have worked out their problems if that man had not stuck his nose in."

"Did he force your mother to call him? And did he insist on her taking his advice?"

"No, but she was vulnerable...."

"Your mother, I assume from meeting you, is an intelligent woman. Am I right? And as an intelligent woman, she made a decision. Is that Nick's fault?"

"I'm telling you, the man is obnoxious and has to be stopped. He's hurting people."

Scott sighed with weariness. "He's only making people think. That's all. His show is followed by people all over this country. It's very successful because he knows just what to say to get people all worked up. Anybody who calls in knows from listening that he's liable to turn them into stuttering idiots or give them unheard-of advice. It's part of the act. But that's all it is. You're overestimating his powers."

"You're *under*estimating them," she snapped. "And if you won't get me an appointment with him, I'll get to him myself."

"For what purpose? He won't think he's done anything wrong."

"To make me feel better. To let him know there are people out there who are appalled at what he's doing."

Scott chuckled. "But don't you see? That's why he's popular. Nobody *likes* Nick Nemoy. Everybody's appalled. That's why they listen. That's why they call in."

"Are you going to get me an appointment with him or not?"

Scott shrugged. "We'll see."

Leslie snatched up her purse and slid back her chair. "I should have known you'd be no help. Take me back to my car, please."

Scott reached for her arm and stopped her from rising. "Wait. I'm just trying to keep you from doing something foolish. Nick isn't what he seems on the radio. He's really a—"

"Don't you dare tell me he's a great guy," she bit out. "He's a disgusting good-for-nothing, and I mean to tell him so. Anybody who gets paid for making people feel small—"

"He gets paid, as I said earlier, for making people think." Scott's face was tight, his eyes eloquent. "He provokes people into mental arguments with themselves, and believe it or not, it helps them to sort out their problems and think about their convictions. Ideas that aren't challenged never ferment into reality. Nick Nemoy challenges everything, and everyone who listens to his show comes away with definite beliefs about something."

"He had no right to challenge my parents' marriage," she said, wondering how she had lost this battle when she'd been so prepared for it.

Scott studied her, then spoke with conviction. "He has every right when your mother calls in and dumps it in his lap. Whether you like it or not, if your parents had been happy together, Nick Nemoy's one-liner wouldn't have been worth a pile of ashes.''

Leslie stared at her empty glass and swallowed. Maybe Scott was right. All she was sure of was the fact that her father was home alone while her mother was on her way to the Virgin Islands. Darn Nick Nemoy! "This evening is quickly becoming unpleasant," she mumbled.

Scott leaned forward and cupped her chin with his hand until she let her eyes drift up to his. "It didn't start out that way," he said. "And it doesn't have to end that way. I'm truly sorry about your parents. I really do hope they work things out, for your sake if not for theirs. But it won't happen tonight. Nothing is going to change tonight, so why don't we just enjoy each other's company and forget all that?''

She breathed out a sigh, wishing his eyes weren't so hypnotic, so absorbing. He did seem like a nice man, after all. And she had nothing against *him*. "I guess it isn't your fault," she said reluctantly. "After all, you aren't the one who called my dad a schmuck.''

The music was soft and nostalgic, the song reminding her of a crush she'd nursed on a football player when she was fifteen. But now she was twenty-five, too old for crushes, and yet the same irrational feelings fluttered in her heart. Scott still held her chin, and unconsciously she wet her lips. "You're so beautiful," he whispered, and this time his eyes held no humor. "Even when you're angry. I could get used to looking at you, Leslie Torrence.''

"You don't even know me," she said, as if it made a difference. "And I don't know you."

"Then we'll just have to work on that, won't we?" When she hesitated, he added, "Honestly, Les. Don't I seem sincere?"

The way he changed her name to suit him stirred her. No one had ever called her Les before, not even Stephen, and it lent a touch of intimacy to their being together. Slowly, she nodded her head. "Yes, you do. But people are not always the way they seem."

A knowing grin crept across his face and he leaned back, draining his wine. Then, holding his empty glass up as if in a toast, he said, "You're a smart lady, Leslie Torrence. A real smart lady."

CHAPTER TWO

LESLIE TRIED TO DISMISS the feeling that Scott Jenkins was laughing at her as he ushered her from the café into the night air, laced with the faint smell of rain. His eyes danced with humor each time she looked at him, and his grin and that dimple seemed carved in his face. It was difficult to look at him and not answer his smile, but she couldn't help wondering if she were merely being pulled into a trap with which he had captured countless others. Scott Jenkins, she was certain, was no amateur when it came to pursuing women.

"I don't suppose you've ever walked around here at night," he said, nodding toward the wooden deck that led behind the café. "You can see all sorts of turtles and frogs, and sometimes you can catch a snake peaking up through the water."

Leslie shivered in the cool moist air. "No, I can't say I've ever done that." She wasn't sure she even cared to.

"Well, then, we'll have to do it now." He took her hand and pulled her onto the deck and around into the shadows behind the building. A few yellow lights attached to the posts lit the view the diners had from the windows of the café. From where Scott and Leslie stood, she could see at least a dozen turtles in the shallow water below them, lit in a golden corral. The sound of wind across water, the occasional splash of a fish and the soft chirp of birds in the trees along the bank added a serene touch to the evening, which seemed nothing more than a fairy tale that would disappear with the turning of a page. "Isn't that great?" Scott asked, leaning his elbows on the railing.

Leslie only smiled and looked at him, watching his eyes sparkle in the darkness. His youthful enthusiasm was refreshing.

"I mean, think about it. How many times have you swum in that water? And I'll bet you've never seen more than one or two of those little devils. I wish I'd brought my camera."

"I've never gone swimming in that water," she said, on the verge of laughter.

"You haven't? Really? Where are you from?"

"Born and raised in New Orleans."

Scott clicked his tongue and shook his head. "Disgraceful. A south Louisiana girl who's never even felt the Mississippi mud oozing between her toes. Lady, you've led a sheltered life."

Leslie gave in and laughed. She leaned on the railing next to him. Their shoulders brushed; their faces were inches apart. She wondered how he'd managed to make her feel so comfortable. "I've never exactly felt deprived of that," she said, her eyes dropping to his lips.

His voice was a deep rumble. "I guess it's hard to feel deprived when you've never had the experience." His arm unfolded from the rail and slid around her back.

Leslie wasn't sure just what his words implied, but a warning bell went off in her head and she started to pull away. Before she could move, however, he had slung his other arm under her legs and scooped her up. She screamed as he leaned forward, holding her over the rail, as if threatening to drop her into the water. She threw her arms around his neck, squeezing for dear life. When her face was buried in his neck, he pulled her back. She could hear his deep laughter against her ear.

"There now," he said, looking down at her. "I finally got you where I want you. Clinging to me like there's no tomorrow."

And before she could answer, his lips had claimed hers. She thought of pulling away, but as his tongue invaded the warm recesses of her mouth and coaxed her into response, the idea fled. Without breaking the bond of their lips, he set her on her feet, sliding his hand up her thigh, over the wrinkled cloth of her skirt, up her hip and rib cage, beneath her blazer. His other hand worked in her hair, removing bobby pins and letting them drop between the planks beneath them. When her hair broke free and fell about her shoulders, he pulled back and looked at her. "Just as I thought," he whispered, then pulled her against him and kissed her again.

Leslie felt herself trembling. He took one of her hands from behind his neck and moved it down his muscular chest to his heart. She felt it racing against her palm, beating out an unmistakable message. His arms wrapped tightly around her. She knew she could lie down and make love to this man without a second thought, and the knowledge terrified her. Never before had any man so thoroughly robbed her of control. Not even Stephen.

His lips tore away from hers, and his heavy breath led her to want more. "Who are you, Leslie Torrence?" he whispered into her hair.

"I was wondering the same thing about you," she murmured.

He slid his hands to her waist and held her apart from him, but he still caressed her with intimate sweeps of his eyes. "You're a vision. I'll dream about you tonight. Standing here in the shadows, all dressed in white, with this beautiful hair draped around your face. Come home with me so you'll be more than a dream."

She took his hands from her waist and stepped back. "No. I can't go home with you. Not tonight."

"Tomorrow night?" he asked. The only stars visible were those shining in his eyes.

She shook her head.

"The next night?"

"Are you asking me to go out with you or sleep with you?"

He tilted his head and grinned in the seductive way that had delighted her all evening. "I guess I'm asking for whatever you'll give me. Like I said earlier, I only take what I'm offered."

She narrowed her eyes and smiled up at him, unwilling to give an answer until the question was more specific.

He lifted her hand and kissed the palm. "Leslie Torrence, will you consider having dinner with me tomorrow night?"

Leslie wondered if he could see in her eyes what he did to her. She hoped not. She opened her mouth to say yes, but a sudden thought sobered her, as if cold water had been flung in her face. The sparkle in her eyes died. "Can't. I have a date tomorrow night."

His shoulders dropped with the depth of his sigh. "The best ones are always taken." Considering the problem a moment, he cocked a brow. "What night don't you have a date?"

Leslie studied the grain of the ramp, wishing she wasn't committed to Stephen.

When she didn't answer, he tried again. "A week from Tuesday? May twenty-second? July ninth? When?"

She raised her head and looked at him, but still said nothing.

Sliding his hands in his pockets, Scott leaned back on the rail. "Is this one man I'm competing with, or fifty? I can handle either, but I just want to know what I'm up against."

Leslie breathed a laugh. "One man."

Scott nodded with frustration. "The worse of the two evils." He sucked in a breath. "Okay. Are you engaged?"

"We have an...understanding," Leslie said.

He reached out and took her left hand, ran the pad of his callused thumb across her knuckles. "No ring?"

Leslie shook her head. She had been offered one, but the time had not seemed right. She didn't want it until they had set a date.

"Then there's nothing to stop me from stealing you away from him," he said, cocking his head, not dropping her hand.

"Nothing but my good judgment," she answered, the sparkle returning.

He snapped his fingers. "Darn. I never counted on good judgment."

She turned his hand over in hers and shook it. "Count on it," she said with a grin.

"I will," he said, smiling at her platonic gesture. Then he wrapped an arm around her shoulder and turned her toward the car. "But *you* can count on needing it."

She didn't doubt that for a moment, for even as he opened the car door and propped an elbow on the silver top, she felt that judgment slipping. "It's starting to rain," he said, sandwiching her between his hard imposing body and the open door.

She didn't get in immediately, only held out her hands and caught the first few drops. "It's time we had a good storm," she said in a bold whisper. "It's been dry too long."

When she got in, he smiled perceptively and closed the door behind her.

LESLIE LAY IN BED that night listening to the sound of the rain beating against her window. Now and then the darkness of her room was lifted briefly, yielding to a flash of lightning outside the window. Yes, it was high time for a storm in her life, she thought.

The thought had no sooner been recognized then a pang of guilt hit her. She had Stephen. She didn't need anyone else.

For the first time in two years, she wondered if the way Scott had manipulated her heart in a single evening indicated there was a flaw in her relationship with Stephen. She had not been dissatisfied with Stephen. Only...unstimulated. Yes, that was it. She closed her eyes and struggled to recall a moment when Stephen had invoked the passion she had felt tonight with Scott. There was none. The race her heart had run in this virtual stranger's presence was unprecedented in her life.

But what did she know about Scott Jenkins? That he worked for an obnoxious warped man she detested. That he had beautiful perfect teeth. That his dark eyes twinkled when he smiled. That she wished she had touched his hair when he'd kissed her tonight.

Nothing. She knew nothing about him. And yet she was lying in bed, wishing he was beside her, wondering what he would have thought of the thin white nightgown she wore, wondering how it would have felt to have his hands rove over her bare skin beneath the cloth. She closed her eyes and hugged her pillow. What would he have thought of her if just that once in her life she had followed her instincts and gone home with him? Would she have seemed too awkward, too inexperienced?

She tried to forget the way he had tricked her into kissing him, or how his hands had felt moving across her hips. And she tried to hang on to the thought that her security and familiarity and fond relationship with Stephen were more lasting than one breathless moment with Scott. When she saw him again—if she saw him again—she was sure she would find that he wasn't half of what her imagination now conjured up. Storms never lasted long, she told herself. She only hoped she had the chance to find out for certain.

But when she had fallen asleep, she found that lightning invaded it, too. Bright thunderless lightning, and the face of a man she barely knew.

"IF I LOOK at one more ledger I'm going to go crosseyed," Maggie, Leslie's close friend and assistant, said from across the room that served as an office in Leslie's home. "Isn't there anything I can do that doesn't involve numbers?"

"At the end of a quarter, no," Leslie replied as her fingers worked rapidly on her calculator.

Maggie stood and stretched, her long slender body arching like that of a cat. "I'm going to get some coffee. Want some?"

Leslie shook her head and jotted down her totals.

When Maggie returned from the kitchen, she sat on the edge of her friend's desk. "You haven't told me about last night yet, and I was so busy I forgot to ask. Did you meet Nick Nemoy?"

A grin broke out on Leslie's face and she leaned back in her chair. "No. I seem to have missed him. But I did meet a man who works for him. Now, he was very interesting."

"Interesting how?"

Leslie ran the eraser of her pencil along her lower lip. "Just interesting."

"Oh." The word and the knowing look on Maggie's face told Leslie she understood. "I never thought you'd find anyone associated with Nick Nemoy 'interesting.'"

"Neither did I. But he asked me to have coffee with him so I could give him my complaints, and before I knew it, Nick Nemoy was the farthest thing from my mind."

Maggie's mouth fell open. "So what happened?"

"We talked," she said, eyes twinkling with the memory. "He showed me the turtles."

"The turtles?"

Leslie saw the confusion on Maggie's face and laughed. "Never mind." She sighed. "He asked me to have dinner with him tonight, but of course I said no."

Maggie breathed a sigh of relief. "Thank goodness."

"Why?" Her best friend's loyalty to Stephen sometimes annoyed her.

"Because Stephen doesn't deserve that."

She glared at Maggie a moment, watching her sip the steaming coffee as if the whole subject had been settled. "Maggie, we're talking about dinner—not a weekend in the Bahamas."

Maggie slid off the desk and offered a slow grin. "Take it from me. Innocent dinners often lead to weekends in the Bahamas. Not that I disapprove of little romantic sojourns to tropical islands. It's just that I think you're looking in the wrong place."

Leslie shook her head and cast her eyes heavenward. "Maggie, I'm not *looking* at all. One minute I'm telling you about a man I met last night, one I do not intend to have dinner with, and you're lecturing me about running off to the Bahamas!"

The telephone rang as Maggie threw back her blond head and laughed. "Geez, you have trouble staying on the subject," she teased, reaching to answer it. "Torrence, Inc.," she said into the phone, then held the receiver up for Leslie. "Stephen. Beware, he sounds sick."

Leslie took the call on her own desk. "Stephen?"

A sneeze came from the other end, followed by a muffled sound, and then Stephen cleared his throat and answered. "Sorry, Leslie. It's this stupid cold."

"How is it?" she asked absently, punching out a series of numbers on her calculator.

"Terrible. I think my sinuses are infected." He cleared his throat, then sneezed again.

"Wish I could do something," she said, trying to find sympathy for the man who seemed to come down with more illnesses than the ones he studied in his medical classes. "Have you started on an anti-biotic?"

"Yes," he groaned. "And I can't miss any classes. But I'm going to be zapped tonight, so I'm afraid I can't take you to see Max Havard after all."

Leslie leaned back in her chair, her pencil falling onto her desk with a clatter. Her eyes moved to the corner of her desk and the two tickets for the final show of the Las Vegas entertainer in town performing at a hotel in the French Quarter. "Stephen, this is his last night here. It was your idea to see him, and you have no idea what I had to do to get these tickets!"

"Leslie, I'm sick!"

You're always sick, was the thought that almost rolled off her tongue, but a sudden wave of guilty sympathy washed over her. "I know you are," she said with a sigh. "I don't want you to go if you're sick. It's just that I don't know what to do with these tickets. They were very expensive."

"You could take Maggie," Stephen suggested.

"She has a date."

"You could take your father," he tried again.

"He doesn't like to have fun," Leslie said without thinking. "I mean, I don't think he'd enjoy it."

"You could at least ask," Stephen was saying, but Leslie's attention was diverted by the ringing of the doorbell. Maggie went to answer it.

When Leslie heard her assistant's swift intake of breath and the mumbled, "Oh, my God," she stood up, straining to see around the wall, but couldn't. "Stephen, I have to go. I'll talk to dad about it."

"Don't go by yourself!" he said quickly.

"I won't," she promised. "Feel better. Bye."

Hanging up the phone, she hurried to the door. A clown with a painted face, a polka-dotted costume and a handful of helium-filled balloons smiled at her. "You Miss Torrence?" he asked.

"Yes," she answered, moving cautiously toward him.

The clown grinned and gave a slight bow as he extended the balloons to her. She took them, mouth agape. They floated into the house, bobbing and bouncing off one another in a rainbow array of colors, bright bows attached to each one. "A dozen balloons? But who in the world?"

"There's a card," the clown offered. "Would you sign here, please?"

Maggie took his clipboard and signed her name. As the clown went back to his delivery van, she turned to

Leslie, an envious smile in her eyes. "Wow. I think I'm going to cry. A dozen balloons." She grinned at the surprise working at Leslie's face. "Well, aren't you going to read the card?"

Leslie reached up to the card attached to one of the bows and pulled it off. "To last night's dream. From a great guy," she read aloud. She nibbled at her bottom lip and looked at Maggie for a reaction.

"What dream did Stephen have last night?" Maggie asked, awed.

"Not Stephen. Scott. The man I was telling you about."

Maggie took the card and studied it earnestly. Glancing back up at the balloons, then again at Leslie, she frowned. "How can you be sure?"

"Because it's signed, 'a great guy.'"

Maggie caught her breath, unamused. "You don't consider Stephen a great guy?"

"You don't understand," Leslie said on a laugh. "Stephen doesn't consider himself a great guy. At least not the way Scott does, and he refers to the fact on a regular basis." Thoughtful silence filled the room as the two stared at the balloons, wondering what to do with them. "He's original, isn't he? Well, at least they don't need water."

"It's not fair," Maggie said, mocking a pout and going back to her desk. "I go to all the right places to meet all the right men. And mine all turn out to be a bunch of frogs. And you walk into a radio station to tell someone off, and pow! You meet a prince when you've already got one. There's no justice in this world."

Leslie tied the strings to a pencil sharpener and sat down to look at her gift. "Balloons," she said in disbelief.

"Balloons," Maggie repeated. "I'd say you have a problem on your hands."

"I'm going to have to watch out," Leslie agreed. "He's good at this."

Trying to push him out of her mind, she went back to work, but each time she glimpsed the balloons looming near her ceiling, an unaccountable smile worked across her face.

When the phone rang just as Maggie was preparing to leave for the day, Leslie picked it up and answered in her most businesslike voice. "Leslie Torrence."

"Leslie Torrence, Scott Jenkins," a deep voice laced with humor returned.

Leslie straightened in her chair and looked at Maggie. "Scott, hi."

"Did you get any surprises today?" he asked. It sounded as if his mouth was pressed close to the receiver, and the thought caused a shiver to course down her spine.

"Yes," she said, smiling. "No one's ever sent me balloons before. Thank you."

"I tried to hire the Goodyear blimp to fly over your house, but they tell me it's in Kentucky right about now."

Leslie laughed, in spite of Maggie's disapproving expression. "The balloons are fine." Her gaze rested on the tickets still on her desk, and she picked them up, turned them over in her fingers and tapped them on her lips.

"Did they win your heart?" he asked. "If not, I have a few other tricks up my sleeve."

"And if they did?" A flirtatious grin curled her lips.

He paused a moment, and when he spoke she could hear the amusement in his voice. "I still have a few other tricks up my sleeve."

Biting her lips, she let her gaze drift across the room to Maggie, who had narrowed her eyes in mock warning.

"Any chance of your ditching what's-his-name early tonight and thanking me properly for my thoughtfulness?" he asked.

Leslie laughed. "I've already thanked you properly. And his name is Stephen."

"Whatever," he said, undaunted. "You could tell him you have to get up early in the morning and get him to bring you home by ten. And then I could—"

"I do have to get up early in the morning," she said, enjoying the way he seemed to find his way around any argument.

"Oh, come on. You aren't the type who has to be in bed by ten-thirty, are you?"

"No, but—"

"But nothing! Has he ever sent you balloons?"

Leslie laughed. "No, you've definitely got him there."

"Then get rid of the guy and have dinner with me. I know this cute little French restaurant that stays open late and—"

Leslie suddenly made up her mind, "Scott, I—"

"Don't say no, yet! I haven't—"

"I wasn't going to say no," she cut in again. "I was just going to tell you that Stephen is sick and I have an extra ticket to Max Havard's final show. Would you like to go with me?"

A long pause followed, and then Scott breathed out a laugh. "Leslie Torrence, I'd love to go with you. But I have to work until ten. We could still catch the second set. Now, as I see it, you have a choice. You could go with someone a lot less interesting and irresistible than I am and see the whole show, or you could see half of it and still have me."

"Wow. What a choice. I guess there's nothing to even think about then, is there?" she asked.

"Of course not," Scott said with perfect assurance. "I'll pick you up at ten-fifteen. And wear your dancing shoes. The night won't end with Max Havard."

Leslie chuckled as she hung up the phone. "I really don't know what to think of this guy," she told Maggie.

"Well, if you must have this little fling, at least realize that somewhere under all that charm, there's probably a frog," Maggie advised. "I've met a lot of them, and this one has all the symptoms. Are you going to tell Stephen?"

Leslie didn't hesitate. "Of course, I'll tell him. I'm not sneaking around. After tonight I'll likely never see Scott again. He probably is a frog under all that charm. Besides, Stephen told me not to go to the Havard show alone."

Maggie only cocked a brow and gathered her work to take home.

Leslie took hours preparing for her date. The anticipation of more of what she had tasted the night before motivated her to attain perfection. She dressed in a turquoise dress with a cowl neck that draped low across her breasts and revealed much of her back, as well. The skirt clung to her hips, offering her both sophistication and sex appeal. Looking in the mirror, she saw that the color drew out the dark flecks buried in the green of her eyes. She wondered if he would notice. But at nine o'clock, when she answered her ringing phone, her thoughts were refocused. It was her mother calling from San Juan.

"I just wanted to tell you that I'm having a wonderful time," her mother said over the feeble connection. "Be sure and tell that schmuck you call your father that for me. Tell him I'm surrounded by wealthy Latin men, and that I may decide to stay here for a few years."

"Mother, please. Call and talk to dad yourself. You've been married too long to just end it all. I know

you can work this out. There's such a thing as compromise, you know."

"Compromise? I've compromised for thirty years.
Do you see him compromising?"

"Mom, he's lonely without you."

"How can you tell?"

Leslie thought a moment. "He hardly talks to anyone. He just loses himself in working on those cabinets."

"So what else is new? Face it, honey. He's not going
to change. So I am. Anyway, I have to go now. I'll call
when we reach the first port."

Leslie slammed down the phone and cursed Nick
Nemoy all over again. Darn that man. Thirty years of
marriage down the drain after a one-minute phone
call. Thirty years of love and respect, and now he had
her mother calling her father a schmuck. *My father is
not a schmuck!*

Deciding to try to reason with her father since she
had failed with her mother, Leslie grabbed her purse
and darted out of the house. She'd meet Scott at the
station. She'd have to get there before the show went
off the air, so they wouldn't miss each other. That
should give her just enough time to tell her father
about the Latin men buzzing around his wife. Maybe
a little jealousy would set a fire under him, she
thought.

But it was of no use. She found him alone in his
workshop behind the house, sanding long strips of
wood. When she had related the conversation to him,

he merely shook his head. "I can't imagine what's got into that woman," he said.

"Dad, she's trying to take drastic action to get your attention. Are you willing to lose her to some South American tycoon?"

Sam took his pipe from his mouth and considered the idea for a moment. "If that's what she wants," he said finally.

"Then dammit, maybe you are a schmuck!" she blurted.

Her father's eyes flashed, full of harnessed temper. "What did you say?"

Leslie wilted in her chair. "I'm sorry. I didn't mean that. But you are a very difficult man to reason with. If you have any desire to keep your marriage to-gether, you'll catch the first plane to San Juan and take that cruise with mom."

"And spoil all her fun?" he mumbled.

Clenching her teeth in exasperation, Leslie slid off her stool. "I give up," she said. She glanced at her watch, then back at Sam who stared at the piece of wood in his hands. "I'd probably ram my head into your wall for a couple more hours if I didn't have a date, but since I do, I'll leave you alone with your cabinets."

"Stephen's taking you out at ten o'clock at night? Wearing that? Don't you have to work tomorrow?"

"Dad, I'm twenty-five years old, and you don't have to worry about how late I stay out. And I'm not going with Stephen. I'll call you tomorrow." Before her father could respond, she was out of the door, swearing under her breath at the stubbornness of the man who had raised her.

Leslie doubted she would get the opportunity to see Nick Nemoy tonight, but she promised herself that if she did, she would go through with telling him off. After all, he was the one who had triggered all her parents' troubles. She knew nothing she said to him would make any difference, but maybe it would make it a little harder for him to sleep tonight. And it would make her feel a great deal better.

The reception area was empty again when Leslie walked into the station. From the speaker overhead, she could hear the fast, sarcastic voice of the host. A young man in a black sleeveless T-shirt and tight jeans passed the door in the hallway and, seeing her, backed up and stuck his head in the lobby. "Can I help you?"

Leslie smiled and moved toward him. "Yes. I'm here to meet Scott Jenkins. We're going out after the show."

The man, no older than twenty, she decided, smiled and nodded. "I'm Larry Rothe, the deejay who takes over after the show." He shrugged and made a come-this-way motion with his head. "I guess you can come on back, since he's expecting you."

Leslie decided not to correct the misconception. She followed Larry down the long carpeted hall, listening as the last caller proclaimed that an angel had told him the president of the United States was, in reality, the biblical beast.

As Nick milked the caller for everything he was worth, Larry opened the door to the studio and ushered her in. The outer room was dimly lit, with cold tiled floors and walls lined with albums. A few folding chairs were pushed against the walls, and to the side was the control booth enclosed in a panel of glass. She looked in and caught her breath when she saw Scott Jenkins, feet propped up on the control panel in front of him, speaking into the mouthpiece attached to the headphones he wore. No one else was in sight.

"Oh, please," he was saying and, dumbfounded, she could hear his words through the speaker, "If there are any more doomsdayers out there, do me a favor and make your calls to Billy Graham or Dear Abby. I have a weak stomach. Until Monday, this is Nick Nemoy, signing off." He punched a button and his theme music began to play. Larry opened the door to the booth, and Scott turned around. All color rushed from his face when he saw Leslie frozen behind the window. He mouthed an expletive, then in one swift movement darted through the door. Enraged, she started out of the room, but he caught her in the hall and swung her around to face him.

"You could at least let me explain," he said, his slower southern drawl slipping back into his speech.

"Liar," she said, jerking her arm from his grip. "I hope you enjoyed it. I hope you found me an amusing toy."

"I wasn't toying with you," he said, grabbing both her shoulders. "I like you and I knew you hated Nick Nemoy. So I just decided not to tell you who I was."

"Deceiving, conniving..." She searched her vocabulary for a suitable word, but came up with only, "Schmuck!"

Scott tried not to smile, but she could see the amusement tugging at the corners of his mouth. "Okay, I deserve that," he said. "What else do I deserve? Get it all out. Just let me have it."

"I'll let you have it, all right," Leslie said, drawing back her fist and crashing it into Scott's face. The impact knocked him off balance, and he immediately grabbed his jaw and covered the fistprint. A flash of anger burned in his eyes, then disappeared.

"Okay," he said calmly, holding out a hand to keep her at a distance. "I guess that was bound to happen sooner or later. What else would you like to do? Drive bamboo shoots under my fingernails? Break my thumbs? I'm at your mercy."

She glared at him, green flames burning in her eyes. She wanted to grab his collar and slam him against a wall, but she doubted she was strong enough. "Nobody plays with me like that! You didn't have to lie to me!"

He pushed a hand through his thick blond hair. "Yes, I did. If I hadn't, you never would have gone out with me. I figured I'd take you out a few times, let you get to know the real me, maybe even make you like me, and then I'd tell you I'm Nick Nemoy."

"You figured it that way, huh? Tell me, who are you really? Nick or Scott? And which one of those accents is yours? The smart-aleck fast-talking clipped one, or the slow, lazy southern one?"

Scott sighed. No trace of amusement showed in his eyes. "I'm really Scott Jenkins. Nick Nemoy is just my name on the show. And this is how I really am. Take it or leave it."

"I'll leave it, thank you very much," she said, storming down the hall.

He followed at her heels. "But we had a date! I dressed up and combed my hair and everything!"

Leslie spun at the door. "Then you and Nick have dinner! I've always heard three's a crowd!"

"But Nick's a lousy dancer!" Scott shouted after her as she dashed out into the night.

Without bothering to retort, Leslie climbed into her car, and screeched out of the parking lot.

CHAPTER THREE

LESLIE SLAMMED THE FRONT DOOR of her house so hard that the paintings on the wall trembled. Headlights illuminated her front window, and she heard Scott cut off the engine and his car door slam. Flicking on the light in the room that served as her office, she saw the bouquet of balloons floating in the air from where they were tied to the pencil sharpener, and the sight was like fuel splashed onto a blazing bonfire.

The doorbell rang, and an urgent knock followed. Trembling with rage, Leslie detached the balloon bouquet, gripping the knotted strings in her fist, and flung open the door. As if she didn't see him she pushed past Scott, the balloons bouncing off him. He pushed them out of his way and followed her to the middle of the yard, where she stood untying the strings so the balloons could separate. Then, with an angry thrust, she released them into the night wind, biting her bottom lip with suppressed rage as they took flight.

"Aw, Les," Scott said, grabbing the string of one balloon that had been stopped by the branch of a tree. "Why'd you have to go and do that?"

She started to turn away, but he grabbed her wrist. Jerking it free, she rushed back into the house, but Scott followed her. "I'm giving you five seconds to get out of my house," she shouted when they were in her office. Scott slammed the door behind him. "Lousy trespasser!" she added.

Scott rubbed his mouth to cover his grin, but it had already spread to his eyes. "I love it when you call me names," he said.

Leslie closed her eyes and tried to concentrate on controlling her temper. First step, relax the hands. Second step, breathe normally. Third step, count to ten. Neither physical nor verbal violence had worked, so now she would try being calm and cool. She held her hands out, palms down, emphasizing her calmness. "All right," she said in a steady voice. "I'm not going to get angry."

"I can see that," he said, sitting on the edge of her desk.

She opened her eyes. "Why did you follow me home?"

He tilted his head and looked at her with a serious glint in his dark eyes. "Because we have a date tonight."

"Had," she corrected. "But the joke's over. I stumbled on the punch line, and you got your laugh. So now that it's over, why are you here?"

He tapped his foot on the carpet and folded his arms. For the first time tonight, she noticed what he wore—camel-colored slacks and a sports coat several shades darker. His off-white shirt was open at the neck, revealing golden curls of hair on his chest. "I didn't ask you out for a joke," he said. "I wanted to take you out because I like you. You're different."

Leslie cocked her brows in disbelief. "Different? How do you know? We just met yesterday. At least half of the conversation we had was a lie. So how can you presume anything about me?"

His jaw popped and she saw him swallow. "I know women," he said. "Let's just say I've had a lot of experience with them."

A humorless breath stole through Leslie's lips. "I never doubted that for a moment," she said. She pulled Maggie's chair out from under her desk and sat down, unwilling to lead him into the living part of her house.

"Look at you," he said, sweeping a hand in her direction. "The way your hands move when you talk, the way your little chin pops up when you're trying to keep your dignity, the way your eyes talk when your mouth won't." His gaze swept caressingly over her body, and his voice lowered a degree. "Just look at you."

Leslie dropped her eyes to the low cut of her dress and hated herself for being so readable. "You came up with all that from spending one hour with me? Come on, Scott. I've had some experience with men, too. I've heard smooth lines before."

He shrugged. "You see? You don't believe someone could actually like you immediately. You're absolutely unaware of your power over men."

Leslie rubbed her temples and sighed. "If that's true, I wish I could use that power to get you out of my house."

Scott stood up and glanced at his watch. His other hand was in his pants pocket, and his coat was pushed back behind his wrist. She noted the lean taper of his waist and the narrow line of his hips. With self-reproach, she willed herself to stay angry.

"Max Havard's second set starts at ten-thirty. Are you coming or not?" he asked.

Leslie only stared at him, exasperated. "How many times do I have to tell you? No! No! No! I'm not going there or anywhere else with you!"

He sank down in a chair and rubbed his chin. "Damn, you're stubborn."

"I'm stubborn? You're the one who's parked in my house and refuses to leave."

He shrugged off his sports jacket and tossed it onto her desk. Slowly, as if trying to keep his temper in check, he began rolling up the sleeves of his shirt, revealing the hard twisting muscles of his forearms. "I want to be here when you change your mind."

Leslie's laugh was dry, unamused. "You expect hell to freeze over soon, do you?"

Appreciation replaced the hint of anger in his eyes, and before she could protest, he stood up and wrapped his arms around her, making her gasp and squirm for freedom. "You are so cute when you're sassy," he said in a deep, intimate rumble.

Leslie felt her cheeks burning with a discomfiting mixture of surprise, arousal and anger, and pressed her hands on his chest to shove him away. When she was free of him, she pushed through the swinging door leading to her kitchen and made a fuss out of getting some aspirin. She turned back to Scott, who watched her while he untied the knot in the surviving balloon he held and raised the opening to his lips. She turned away and washed the aspirin down.

Scott's voice came in a fast Donald Duck cadence when the helium had filled his lungs. "Leslie Torrence, I get the feeling you don't like me."

The absurd sound of his voice took her by surprise, and she gasped, choked on the water, then collapsed against the counter, coughing.

Scott was behind her in an instant, patting her back and getting her more water. When she was breathing normally again, he took her shoulders and gazed into her watery eyes.

"I knew I made you breathless, but I didn't mean to kill you," he said.

Leslie's guard had dropped and she had no strength left to fight him. The humor of the situation slowly overtook her and she gave in to it, letting a smile spread to her eyes. She sighed defeatedly and looked up at him.

"There now," he said in a whisper, running a finger along her bottom lip. "That's what I've been waiting for. Just a smile. A flash of sunshine. It wasn't so much to ask.''

And before she could answer, his lips were on hers. For a moment, she knew the taste of the sunshine he spoke of. His lips were soft, warm, taking only what she gave him, arousing her to offer more. Her lips parted and their tongues came together in slow exploration, learning each other. She felt her breath being drawn from her, and wondered what else she had surrendered in this single kiss. She was afraid to find out. His arms wrapped more tightly around her, and she longed to hold him and mold his face with her hands and slide her fingers through his wheat-colored hair. But instead she kept her hands motionless on the hard rounded muscles of his biceps, for she feared that if she let herself become too familiar with this man who had the power to melt her bones, it would lead to total abandon and draw her completely beyond the point of control. And for Stephen's sake, if not her own, she had to hold on to that control.

She broke the kiss and pulled back to look at him. "I'm not angry anymore," she said honestly. She took a deep fragile breath and slipped out of his arms. "But I really think it's time you went home."

He heaved a frustrated sigh and raised his hands to his hips. "Les, you can't deny the attraction we have for each other."

She shook her head. "No, I can't deny it. I am attracted to you. But I have very distinct ideas about what I want in a man. And you simply don't fit those ideas. I don't like what you do for a living, and I don't like what you represent. And I like to think that my practical side is stronger than the side of me that acts on instincts and emotion. Physical attraction is not enough."

Scott's face became taut and his jaw hardened. His eyes frosted over with understanding. "It must be lonely in that ivory tower of yours," he said.

Somewhere, on a level beneath intellect, his words struck a painful chord.

He walked back into the office and picked up his coat. "I'll go now," he said, heading for the door.

She followed him, fighting the disappointment that he had not challenged her statement, struggling to convince herself it was the best thing. When he had opened the door, he stepped out into the night and turned back to her. Shadows hid his features, but his expression was clear in his voice. "It could have been good, Les," he said, then disappeared in the dark shadows of the trees and got into his car.

As he pulled away, Leslie closed the door and leaned against it, feeling a gnawing void within her she had never felt before.

LESLIE TURNED OVER in her bed and groped for her alarm clock. Two-thirty. Moaning, she slipped out of bed and went to the window to look out at the rain that had begun again. The drops exploded as they hit the glass, then ran down the window, in blurred rivulets. She pressed her forehead against the pane and watched her breath become a misty fog on the glass. *I'm alone,* she thought suddenly, and the realization was crushing.

Turning back to her bed, she flicked on the lamp and sat. The room was bathed in a dim yellow light, and her shadow loomed against the opposite wall like a disproportioned figure in a nightmare. Leslie pulled her knees up to her chin and hugged them, wondering what had brought on the feeling of loneliness. Was it the storm? No, she decided. She had been alone during hurricanes and tornadoes and had never experienced the hollow feeling eating at her now.

She caught her reflection in the mirror and sat up, trying to analyze herself. Her hair fell about her shoulders in a wild unbrushed mop, giving her the appearance of someone who felt rather than someone who thought. She tucked her feet beneath her and looked down at her body hidden beneath the silky white nightgown she wore. Twenty-five years old and still untouched, she thought as she ran a hand over a full breast and down to her stomach. Was that because her morals were too high, as she had told Stephen on many occasions, or because she had never been properly aroused?

She wet her lips and pushed back her hair, wondering what Scott really thought of her. Wasn't she just one more challenge among many? She thought of his eyes, the way they had looked the first time he had kissed her and pulled her hair down and said, "Just as I thought." The memory of his dark probing eyes made the tips of her breasts strain against the soft fabric. She remembered the emotion in those eyes tonight, when he had touched her lower lip and called her smile a flash of sunshine. She wondered if he'd told anyone else that. She wondered if he stood in front of the mirror each morning and practiced that sincere expression while he shaved.

Attraction, she thought. She had told him physical attraction wasn't enough. But wasn't there more? She thought of Stephen, who stood tall and lean and dark, his gray eyes a front for the distracted thoughts that always seemed to be scurrying through his mind. She had always considered him physically attractive, as other women had before her and had since, but that attraction had never kept her awake at night. The only times she had lost sleep over Stephen was when he had pressed her to set a date for their marriage. So what was it about Scott that kept her from sleeping now?

She thought of the things he'd said tonight, the way he had broken down her anger and forced her to fight herself to keep from laughing. She thought of the balloons and his persistence and his smile. And then she thought of the hard lines of his body and the way his arms had felt around her and the taste of him.

Drat, she thought, falling into her pillow. He was the exact opposite of what she wanted in a lover. The exact opposite of Stephen. So why was he haunting her this way? She squeezed her eyes shut and tried to concentrate on the fact that she'd never have to see him again. He had been angry when he'd left. Maybe even hurt. She remembered what he'd said about her ivory tower. There had been little left for her in his eyes when he'd walked away. The struggle was over. She had won. Or had she?

"I TOLD YOU he was a frog," Maggie said the next morning when Leslie related the story of the night before. "But I can't believe the man who swept you off your feet was Nick Nemoy." She giggled into her hands.

"He didn't sweep me off my feet," Leslie clipped. "And I don't think it's funny."

Maggie sat at her desk, cluttered with open ledgers and tax tables. "Well, maybe it taught you a lesson," she said. "Against Nick Nemoy, Stephen certainly seems a lot more desirable. Right?"

Leslie finished the form she had been working on and cleaned off her desk before pulling out another file, wondering if Maggie's comment was indeed true. The sudden realization that it wasn't, gave her a fresh surge of guilt that she hadn't yet told Stephen of the events of the previous night. "At least Stephen has never lied to me," she said quietly.

"Course," Maggie said with a cocky grin, "I haven't seen Stephen make you smile lately the way that guy did yesterday."

Leslie slapped her hand on her desk. "Whose side are you on? Just when I think you're fighting for Stephen, you change sides."

Maggie laughed. "I like a good drama. And I haven't seen you all worked up like this since, well, since Nick Nemoy called your father a schmuck!"

Leslie's face reddened at the reminder. "All right. I made a mistake. I'll admit I was charmed by him at first. It won't happen again, and I intend to tell Stephen all about it, as soon as I talk to him."

"Need to clear your conscience, huh? Did something happen that you haven't told me about?"

Leslie thought of the kiss and the way her body had responded. Immediately she shook her head. "No. And I think this subject has about worn itself out, don't you agree?"

"Okay," Maggie said, punching at her calculator. "For someone with a clear conscience, you sure are touchy."

Before Leslie riposted, the doorbell rang. "It's probably Mr. Jackson with his week's tickets," she said, thankful she'd been saved from further conversation. "I'll get it."

"Saved by the bell," Maggie mumbled as she went back to work.

Leslie waved her off with a smile and opened the door. Immediately her smile faded when she stood face-to-face with Scott Jenkins.

"Scott," she said in surprise. She heard something in the office fall and within seconds Maggie was beside her, peering over her shoulder at the tall blond man carrying a briefcase.

Scott smiled. "May I come in?"

Leslie glanced at Maggie and fumbled for a proper answer. "You know I'm working."

He nodded. "I know. That's why I'm here. It's business."

"Business?"

Maggie pulled her out of Scott's way and held out a hand. "Hi, Scott. I'm Maggie Drummond, Leslie's assistant. Come on in."

Scott shook her hand warmly, and Leslie watched the dimple in his cheek deepen as he strolled into her office. "I didn't know Les had an assistant," he said.

"Les?" Maggie asked, grinning at Leslie, who still stood in the foyer.

Scott's eyes went back to Leslie. She had worn her hair down today, and a strand was caught in her lip gloss. She shoved it back self-consciously and crossed to her desk. Scott had already found a chair. Glancing with annoyance at Maggie, Leslie cleared her throat. "I didn't expect to see you again," she said.

He ran a hand through his hair, only messing it more than the wind already had. "I didn't plan to see you again, either, when I left here last night," he said. His voice was clear, unperturbed at Maggie's presence. He smiled slightly at Leslie, whose face was hidden behind steepled fingers. "But things didn't look so bad this morning, so I decided to forgive you."

As Leslie drew in a breath, she heard Maggie slap a hand over her mouth. "Forgive me? *You* forgive *me*?"

Scott sat up and leaned forward. His eyes danced with humor, but his mouth remained serious. "I know, I know," he said, holding out a hand to interrupt her. "The things you said to me last night were pretty strong. But I'm not the type to dwell on things said in anger. There's no need for an apology."

Speechless, Leslie could only stare incredulously at the man seated across from her.

Maggie stood up. "Uh, I think I'll go make some coffee." Leslie caught the other woman's smile as she pushed through the door to the kitchen.

"I wasn't planning an apology—" she began.

"Good," Scott interrupted. "Then we can get right down to business." He set his briefcase on his lap and opened it, shifting Leslie's attention from disbelief to curiosity.

"We don't have any business together," she objected.

He pulled out a stack of files and dropped them on her desk. "You do have a bookkeeping service, don't you?"

"Well, yes, but—"

"I'd like to hire you," he said.

Leslie didn't take her eyes off him as she reached for the files. "To do what? I work for businesses, not individuals."

He nodded and pointed toward the files. "There are three small businesses there whose books are in bad shape."

Leslie dropped her eyes to the files, then studied Scott again. The humor had faded from his eyes, and he rubbed his lip with the length of an index finger. "Are these your businesses?"

He nodded. "Surprised?"

"A little."

He leaned forward, settling his elbows on his knees. "When you look at those files, you'll see that I desperately need help keeping the books. I'm not a mathematical person, and I hate keeping up with all that stuff. Besides," he said, his eyes locking into hers and refusing to let go, "this way, maybe we can get to know each other a little better. Maybe I can show you that I'm much more than Nick Nemoy."

Leslie swallowed and glanced at the files. "Jim's Auto Accessories?"

He laughed. "It's a long story, but the gist of it is that my brother was having trouble so I bought him out. Don't know a thing about cars, but he runs the place and I take care of inventory and bills and all. I've been a little neglectful keeping the taxes filed right, though, and the government's starting to get a little impatient with me."

Leslie studied him for a moment, trying hard not to let her amusement at his nonchalance break through the reserve she vowed to maintain. She dropped her eyes to the next file. "A Chinese restaurant?"

He nodded. "And I don't even like Chinese food."

"Then why...?"

"It was going under and I knew the owner from school. He talked me into buying it and getting someone else to run it. What can I say? So far the profits have been pretty good."

She looked at the next file. "What's this?" she asked, while she shuffled through receipts and blank overdue tax forms.

"My hobby," he said. "Photography. Occasionally, I sell to a magazine, and now and then someone buys a print. I meant to impress you the other night by showing the prints I have displayed at Morgan's, but I forgot. Usually, my costs absorb my profit, but as you can see, I don't keep up with any of it very well. I'm pretty busy with the everyday problems of keeping up with all this, so I need someone to take care of payroll and taxes."

She sighed and lifted icy eyes to him. "Well I can see that you do need a bookkeeper, but I'm not sure I can take you as a client. My load is pretty heavy now," she said.

Maggie burst through the door, not even pretending she hadn't been eavesdropping. "Don't let her fool you, Mr. Jenkins—or is it Nemoy?"

"Scott," he said grinning.

Perplexed, Leslie glared at Maggie, wondering what on earth had caused her sudden turnabout when she'd been convinced Scott was "a frog." The reference to his being Nick Nemoy made it obvious that Leslie had been talking about him, a bit of ammunition she was not anxious for Scott to have. Biting her lip, she silently vowed to deal with Maggie later.

Maggie ignored Leslie's eloquent eyes and focused on Scott. "We're only this busy because it's the end of the quarter and time for annual taxes. In a few weeks, we'll barely have enough to pay my salary."

Leslie stood up and leaned across the desk. "Maggie, I'll decide—"

"Come on, Les," Scott cut in. "I need help. I'm no good with this stuff. I'd much rather spend my time doing research for my show or playing in a darkroom than at a calculator."

"A darkroom?" she asked, shamelessly letting the image of two lovers in a dark room enter her mind.

Scott grinned with comprehension, and his incorrigible dimple popped back into focus. "A darkroom. Photography, remember?"

Leslie felt her face reddening. "I knew what you meant." Her eyes flashed to Maggie, who quickly went to her desk and began shuffling papers, struggling to keep a smile off her face. "I just don't think—"

"Well, if you can't take the extra load, I'll be glad to," Maggie said brightly, as if she could clear her schedule for Scott as easily as she cleared a spot on her desk.

Leslie's eyes shot green flames at her friend. "Maggie, you don't have any more time than I do." She turned back to Scott. "I'm sorry. We just can't take you right now."

Scott's grin disappeared and she noticed the same tightness he had worn when he'd left the night before. "Don't tell me. You have very high standards about the kind of businesses you'll take, and mine don't fit into that mold."

The picture he painted of her, no matter how inaccurate, made her uncomfortable. Maggie opened her mouth to speak again, and Leslie knew she had been defeated. "All right!" she clipped. "I suppose I can fit you in. I could use the business. But I don't have time to look over it all right now. We'll have to talk about this more in depth, later, so I can see exactly what will be expected of me in this relationship."

His smile returned and he stood. "How about tomorrow? We can have an 'in-depth' discussion then."

She glanced at her calendar. "Tomorrow's Saturday."

"Is that a problem?" he asked. "I thought that would be easier than taking you away from your work on a weekday in the middle of a busy season. It could take a while to go over all this, you know."

She sighed. "All right. Tomorrow morning then. About ten-thirty?"

"Good," he said, following her to the door. She opened it and leaned her shoulder against it, trying to remain unaffected by his direct eyes. "I'm looking forward to our relationship," he said, leaning forward as if to kiss her. She jumped back, and he chuckled and touched her nose. Then he took the doorknob from her and pulled the door shut behind him.

Leslie breathed out a huff of air and collapsed against the door, just before she saw Maggie bury her head in her arms and begin to laugh hysterically.

"When you're finished laughing," she told Maggie in a soft controlled voice, "I hope you will explain to me what on earth has got into you. Not twenty minutes ago, you were reminding me that this guy was no more than a frog in a prince's suit, and that I owe it to Stephen to stay away from him, and the next thing I know—"

"Well, for heaven's sake," Maggie interrupted, unable to erase her smile now that her laughter was under control, "you said the man was interesting but you never told me he was a rich hunk. Who cares if he's a frog when he looks like that?"

Leslie gaped at her, arms akimbo. "Your values never cease to amaze me. Not to mention your audacity! How dare you tell him that we could take him when I had just told him we were snowed under?"

Maggie leaned back, propping her legs on the desk with an unthreatened grin. "I told him *I* would take him. And I would have gladly done so if you hadn't jumped in. It might have taken a little overtime—late nights, early mornings... Of course, I don't blame you. Did you see those eyes?"

A crooked smile broke across Leslie's face, and she wilted against the wall. "Have you changed your mind about Stephen?"

Maggie laughed aloud. "Heck no. I'll take whichever one you decide to give up. Incidently, I think Stephen's more your type. Maybe you should let Scott down easily, and then I'll soothe his ruffled ego. Boy, would I like to soothe his—"

"Maggie!" Leslie said in mock rebuke. "Get back to work."

Shrugging with grand exaggeration, Maggie dropped her feet and scooted to her desk. "You're right. I'll catch him before his heart is broken. That way he'll think it was his idea. I'll let him think it's you he really wants, when it's me all along."

Leslie only smiled and switched on her calculator, pretending disinterest as Maggie babbled on.

CHAPTER FOUR

LESLIE MANAGED to convince herself that her nerves were under perfect control Saturday morning as she dressed. When she finally decided on a pair of jeans and a stiff-collared blouse of white eyelet, unbuttoning it to the faintest hint of her cleavage, she wondered if one of the first four outfits she'd tried on was better suited for her meeting with Scott. No, she decided. She wasn't going to take any more pains for him. He was just a client, and what she had on would have to do. But when the doorbell rang at nine-thirty—a whole hour early—her reserve shattered and fell around her in a million pieces.

"You're early," she said as she opened the door, but her face fell with her heart when Stephen greeted her, laden with an armload of medical books. "Oh, Stephen."

Dropping a kiss on her lips, the tall man stepped inside. "Who were you expecting?" he asked as she closed the door.

"A new client," she said, following him into the living portion of her house. "I didn't have time to go over his books with him this week, so he's coming over today." She watched as Stephen dropped his texts on the couch and sank into a recliner, running his hands through his brown hair. Wondering briefly if he'd gone to great lengths to make it look so unkempt, she asked on cue, "How do you feel?"

"I'll be okay," he said without much confidence. "It seems to have contained itself in my lungs. I've been having severe chest pains and a low-grade fever. My throat is sore and—"

"Aren't those just symptoms of the common cold?" Leslie asked cautiously, though she knew what his answer would be.

"Don't you think I'd know a cold if I had one? No, this is much more serious. My guess is that it's an early stage of pneumonia."

"Probably," Leslie agreed, knowing that arguing about the seriousness of one of Stephen's illnesses was futile and took far more energy than just humoring him. He had been studying respiratory disorders, and it was not unusual for him to actually suffer symptoms as he studied them. He had considered specializing in cardiology, but had changed his mind, for which she was thankful. She doubted his heart would have survived it.

"How about some breakfast?" he asked, taking her hand.

"No thanks, I've already eaten," she answered.

He tried to laugh, but coughed instead. "I mean for me," he said. "I need a nice hot meal. I haven't felt like cooking."

Leslie sighed. "Stephen, I'm really sorry you don't feel good, but I have a business meeting in less than an hour."

"It doesn't take that long to whip up some bacon and eggs," he groaned, pulling on her hand. "I was going to study over here today, but if it's that important I'll leave before your client gets here."

"I thought your throat was sore."

"It is, but at this point I think the nourishment would be worth the pain of choking it down."

"Wonderful," Leslie said, jerking her hand from his and going to the kitchen. "I'll cook and you'll choke it down."

"Oh, come on, Leslie. I didn't mean it that way," he said, standing up. His shirttail hung loosely over his pressed pants, and she wondered again if he had consciously tried to look like a sick person. Rebuking herself, she got out the frying pan and slapped in some bacon. It wasn't his fault. Whether it was in his mind or not, he really did feel ill. It was just that he usually dressed with such care that she found this rumpled untidy state hard to believe.

Glancing at the oven clock, she saw that it was nine forty-five. If she could cook the meal in ten minutes, and Stephen "choked it down" in fifteen, then took ten to groan a little more and complain about having to study at home, maybe he would be gone before Scott arrived. Heaving a guilty sigh as she cooked, she considered telling Stephen about Scott. But what was there to tell? Scott was just a client, and she had already told him that. The date she had planned with him had ended before it began, so there was no reason to get Stephen worked up over it. She had told him all there was to know, she convinced herself as she set the table for one.

"Aren't you eating with me?" Stephen asked when he sat down.

Leslie lowered into the chair across from him, her stomach queasy with the fear that he wouldn't leave before Scott arrived. "I told you I'd already eaten."

"I thought you were kidding," he said, digging in.

Irritated, Leslie crossed her arms on the table and frowned. "Why would I kid about it, Stephen?"

He gave a hurt shrug and shoved the eggs around on his plate. "If I'd known you were serious, I wouldn't have asked you to cook. Sorry."

Another wave of guilt washed over her as she reproached herself for being so unsympathetic. After all, he was used to her doing things for him when he didn't feel well. She had never minded before. If only he wouldn't take so long!

"What are you so nervous about?" Stephen asked finally when he'd cleared his plate.

Immediately, Leslie stopped swinging her leg and tapping her fingers. "What do you mean?"

"I mean you're fidgeting. Are you afraid of catching what I've got?"

At first his words made no sense, and she narrowed her eyes in confusion. "Catching what you've got?

Oh, yes. Maybe a little, I guess. I really can't afford to get sick during tax season."

He took her hand in his, squeezed it affectionately. "I can understand that. I'll just be careful not to—"

At that moment the doorbell rang and Leslie jumped completely out of her seat. "He's early!" she shouted. "It's only ten after!"

Stephen laughed. "Relax. You're ready, aren't you?"

Leslie took a deep breath and closed her eyes, wishing she'd open them to find Stephen gone. But he made no move to leave. Silently making an alphabetic list of expletives, she left him in the kitchen and went to the front door. Maybe Stephen wouldn't notice Scott's virility. Maybe Scott wouldn't flirt. And maybe she would turn into a little mouse and vanish beneath the floorboards! Taking a deep breath and trying not to look quite so forlorn, she opened the door.

Scott greeted her wearing nothing but a smile and a pair of cutoff jeans. His tanned skin glistened in the warm sunlight that caressed him through the trees. "I don't believe it," he said, crossing muscular arms and leaning in the doorway. His hair, falling in a soft tumble against his forehead, looked as if he had washed it and let it dry unbrushed. His clear eyes dropped to the opening in her blouse, remaining for only a second, then returned to her face. "You're the only woman I know who can look Victorian and erotic at the same time." His smile faded and his lids lowered a little as he leaned closer to her.

Praying that Stephen couldn't overhear, Leslie stepped back and tried to keep her eyes on Scott's face rather than the hard slopes of his naked chest. "And you're the only man I know who dresses so carefully for a business appointment."

He laughed and glanced down at himself. "Oh, yeah," he said, as if he'd forgotten. "Sorry about this." He ran a thumb down the line of hair from his chest to the waistband of his shorts and straightened. "I did have on a shirt, but I had some car trouble on the way over and it kind of got covered in grease." He shrugged and grinned. "Didn't do me a darn bit of good, either. I don't know enough about cars to do much more than change the oil."

"You mean you would have been earlier?" she asked, astounded.

"No," he said, his dimple becoming a long gash in his cheek. "See, I went to my health club to work out this morning. I had planned to go home and change before I came over here, but by the time I had wheels it was almost ten, so I came straight here."

Leslie glanced through the trees shading her lawn and saw the topless Jeep parked in her drive. "Is that yours?"

He shook his head. "It's my brother's. He knows cars, so I called him and we swapped while he works on mine."

Leslie nodded, her eyes moving over his body despite her efforts to stop them. Thank goodness Stephen *was* here, she thought suddenly. Scott Jenkins was too much for her. It wasn't him she feared as much as herself. She wasn't experienced enough to predict her own reactions to his masculinity.

"Does it bother you?" he asked in a low voice, barely penetrating her thoughts. He raised his elbow, leaning it on the jamb and cocked his head, looking down at her. She tore her gaze from his body and met his eyes.

"Of course not. It's just that, well, I'm not used to my customers keeping their appointments half naked. It's a bit, uh, distracting."

"I know the feeling," he rumbled, dropping his eyes to her chest again. "Now are you going to let me in, or do you have some rule about men being fully dressed before entering your house?"

"The idea never occurred to me until now, but maybe it would be a good idea," she replied.

He leaned closer to her, and she smelled the fresh scent of soap and felt the warmth of his skin as her folded arm pressed into his hard stomach. She moved her arm and slid her hand into her back pocket, her eyes locking directly into his. She swallowed.

"Get the files and come with me," he said almost intimately.

The soft order seemed alien, and the words made no sense in the context of the moment. "What?" she asked from her daze of hypnotic attraction.

His closeness to her and the hold of his eyes did not alter. "Get my files and we'll talk about them at my place. I can change at home and then we can get right to work."

"She's not going anywhere with you," Stephen said from the doorway of the foyer, and Leslie spun around like a child who'd been caught stealing from the cookie jar.

Stephen's posture had straightened considerably, and his hands held his hips as if he were ready to draw a pistol. His mouth was a flat slash across his face, and Leslie winced uncomfortably.

"Uh, Scott, this is Stephen Tate, my...boyfriend."

If Scott was perturbed by his adversary's sudden appearance, he didn't show it in the powerful, graceful way he thrust out a hand and stepped toward Stephen. But she could see the hard muscles of his tanned back rippling with tension as the two men stood face-to-face, Scott's hand turned palm downward as he continued to offer it despite Stephen's resistance.

Fianlly, as if he didn't know what else to do, Stephen took it and shook. "So this is your client," he mumbled with special emphasis on the last word. "What kind of work is it that you expect to do with my fiancée, Mr....?"

"Jenkins," Scott supplied coldly. "What kind of business does your fiancée—" he made a special effort to put emphasis on *fiancée* "—usually do with her clients?"

Stephen lifted his chin and peered down his long nose at Scott. His pale face was reddening. Wondering if she should intervene, Leslie moved up beside the two men. When Stephen's nostrils flared and the veins in his neck strained against the skin there, she braced herself for him to strike. Instead, he brought his chin down, raised his hand to his face and let out a sneeze that made her jump.

Scott didn't smile as she would have predicted, but the expression in his face became somewhat lighter as his body relaxed. "Bless you," he said in that insufferable drawl, then turned back to Leslie. "Are you ready to go?"

"Wait for me in the Jeep," she said finally. "I'll get the files."

Scott nodded consent, then turned back to Stephen. "Nice meeting you," he said. "You take care of that cold, now." And then, sliding his hands into his tight back pockets, he sauntered out the door to the waiting Jeep.

"If you think I'm going to let you leave this house with that man," Stephen said through clenched teeth, "you are sadly mistaken."

Leslie went into her office to get Scott's files. "We would stay here," she told him when she emerged, "but under the circumstances I think things would be a little uncomfortable."

"Why? Because I'm here? The third wheel?"

Leslie blew out an annoyed breath. "Stephen, I'm a businesswoman. I'm not accustomed to having a chaperon for my business meetings."

Stephen pointed to the door that Scott had just walked through. "If you think that guy has business on his mind, then you're more naive than I thought you were! You are not going with him!"

"I already have a father, Stephen," she said calmly. "I accept his opinions, but I don't always follow them. I don't intend to change that policy with you." Grabbing her purse off the table beside the door, she walked outside.

"I'm warning you, Leslie. Don't go with him!"

"And I'm warning you," she bit out, turning to face him. "When it comes to my business, your intrusions are not welcome. I don't get involved with your diagnoses, and you will not get involved in my accounts. If you want to continue having a relationship, you'd better learn that now. Lock the door when you leave." Closing the door behind her, she heard a loud thud within the house and prayed nothing had been broken.

Scott's dark eyes watched her approach the Jeep, and when she got in, she set the files on the floor and turned to him. "I'm sorry Stephen was rude. I didn't expect him to show up this morning. He hasn't been feeling well and he's under a lot of pressure at med school."

"Can't say I blame him," Scott said, cranking the engine and backing out of the driveway. "If I were in his place I'd fight like hell to keep you."

Leslie breathed a heavy sigh. "Scott, I'm telling you what I told him. This is a business meeting. Nothing else."

Scott's silky blond hair flapped around his face as he drove, and he glanced over at Leslie. "Still. A man knows when his territory is becoming shaky."

"I am not his territory, and our relationship is not shaky!" she shouted over the road noise.

Scott stopped for a red light. Leaning toward her as he waited for it to change, he said in an intimate voice, "I've kissed you, remember? A woman who's committed to a man doesn't respond like that in someone else's arms."

"The light is green," Leslie clipped, holding her hair to keep it from whipping her face.

As the Jeep began moving again, Scott glanced her way. "And I'll tell you another thing, Les, just so things will be fair. I'm not going to let up. Old Stevie's got a fight on his hands."

Although his arrogance annoyed her, Leslie couldn't stop the strange thrill coursing through her at his warning. Just the same, she told herself, she had no intention of getting involved with Scott Jenkins or Nick Nemoy or any other form of the man who had turned her life upside down for the past few days. Glancing his way, she noticed his enjoyment of the struggle she was having with her hair, so she dropped her hands and let it fly. By the time they reached his modest ranch-style house at the edge of a beautiful plot of land, her hair was tangled and full around her face.

Reluctantly, she followed him in, noting the masculine feel of each room, from the large living room with oak floors and throw rugs to the adjoining kitchen decked with every modern convenience that could make bachelor life simpler.

"Like it?" he asked, leaning against the counter, still bare chested, looking at her with a fond glint in his eye.

"It looks just like you," she admitted with a smile. The pleasant expression on her face dispelled any doubts he might have had that her remark was sincere. "Did you decorate it yourself?"

He looked around as if seeing the place for the first time. "Is it decorated?"

She laughed. "Of course it is. The prints on the walls, the placing of the rugs, the furniture."

"Oh," he said. "Well, yeah, I guess I did decorate it."

"It's very nice."

"But?" he asked, as if she had more to say.

"But what?"

He shrugged. "Well, you know. Most women, when they come in here, have a little something to say about how it needs a woman's touch."

"Why? You live here, not a woman. I think it suits you perfectly."

He smiled and assessed her with special care as her eyes panned the room. "That's what I always thought," he said. "Would you like to see my dark-room?"

Nodding, she followed him into the small room lit only by a single white bulb. "I built this all myself," he said proudly, running a hand along the dry bench. He pointed to the wet bench on the other side of the room, a long table with a built-in sink and three processing trays on it. "I used to use the bathroom for a darkroom, but it was such a hassle light-proofing the windows and setting everything up over the bathtub every time I needed to use it. Now I can come in here anytime."

Leslie eyed the machinery mounted on the walls. "Why is everything mounted that way?"

"So there won't be any vibration while the prints are processing."

She nodded. "It's so clean. It looks like you haven't used it in weeks."

He grinned. "I used it just last night. It's very important to keep a darkroom clean, because the dust can settle on my enlarging equipment and ruin prints."

"Interesting," she said, looking around. "May I see some of your work?"

"You already have," he said. "Those prints in the living room are mine."

Leslie stepped out of the darkroom and looked at the living-room wall, where an arrangement of matted black-and-white prints was hung. "These are yours?"

"Yes," he said, following her out and closing the door behind him. "Those were taken in my dark period."

"Dark?" she asked, but then she saw the tragedy in the photos and understood. One was a smashed and dirty soft-drink cup on a stretch of soiled pavement. It wasn't the cup, nor the dirt, nor the pavement that made the statement. It was the violence that came from someplace she could not pinpoint, the hopelessness that radiated from the image. Her eyes moved to another photo, and she squinted at first, unsure of what she was seeing, until she realized it was an extreme close-up of a battalian of ants blanketing the corspe of a tiny unidentifiable animal. The next print was a broader shot of a funeral scene, the anguished faces of the mourners clearly visible, and the coffin of a small child being lowered into the ground.

"How did you get that shot?" she asked quietly, not taking her eyes from the picture. "It clearly wasn't staged. This was a real funeral."

"Yes, it was real." His voice startled her, for it was right behind her. She turned and saw the memory in his eyes and the vulnerability in his face.

"Did you know them?"

"No," he said softly. "Not personally."

She looked back to the photo again and felt a tug at her heart at the agonized control on the mother's face. "Why did you photograph it?"

He turned to look at her. "It was something I didn't ever want to forget. I always try to photograph things I need to remember. Feelings that go as easily as they come. Fleeting feelings that shouldn't be fleeting."

For a moment she stared at him in surprise. He was revealing a side of himself she hadn't known existed. But then, she'd met him only a few days ago.... Shaking her head as if to clear it, she said, "You told me these were from your dark period. What period are you in now?"

The sad expression melted and he smiled. "I'm not sure. It's hard to label a period while you're living it. But I know it isn't dark. It's one of the brightest I've known."

The sincerity in his voice and the vulnerability she'd just seen in his face moved her again, and when his full mouth began to lower toward hers, Leslie did not pull away. He was a beautiful man, and she wanted to touch him. The kiss was gentle, achingly so, and his hands moved around her back as carefully as if she were a crystal treasure. He deepened the kiss, and the soft warmth of his tongue against hers pulled needs and desires from her core that she'd never known she had. Her hands, following the lead of her heart, scaled his chest, learning the texture of hair and the softness of skin, passing over the granuled peaks that told her he, too, knew that need and desire. She raised her hands to his neck, felt the pounding pulse by his throat, brushed her fingers through his hair. His arms pressed her more tightly against him, and she felt the hardness of his chest crushing her soft breasts, the tightness of his legs against hers. The intensity of her need consumed her, shook her, terrified her.

She moved her lips away from his and slid her hands back down to his chest, halfheartedly pushing him away as she fought sensations she'd never experienced before. "No," she whispered with the little breath she could find.

"No what?" he breathed, kissing her cheek, then her temple.

She closed her eyes and moaned. "Why does this happen every time I'm with you?"

"We can't help ourselves," he whispered against her neck. "The first time I saw you, I knew you'd drive me crazy, and you do. Absolutely, irreversibly, incurably crazy."

"But I haven't done anything," she said in feeble protest.

"You don't have to do anything," he said. "Not one thing. All you have to do is stand there and I nearly lose control." As he framed her face with his hands and gazed down at her, Leslie knew he had branded her soul with his look, printed her skin with his hand, marked her lips with the forceful softness of his own. It would be very, very hard, she knew, for her ever to be quite the same again.

He took a deep breath and stepped back, sliding his fingers down her bare arms until he reached her trembling fingers. "But I will control myself," he said with a half smile.

She didn't answer, staring at him with emerald eyes so round and full of emotion that she didn't have to speak. He swallowed and dropped her hands. "Maybe it isn't such a good idea for us to work in here," he offered.

"You could get dressed and we could go back to my house." Her voice was hoarse, shaky. "I'm sure Stephen has gone by now."

He grinned. "You drive me just as crazy at your house as you do here."

She dropped her eyes, felt heat scorching her face, looked away.

"I'll tell you what," he said, running his spread fingers through his hair. "How about if we work out on the sundeck?" He released a breath, his uncertainty revealed in the crooked smile on his face. "Being out in the open will maybe help me keep my hands to myself. Besides, it's been raining for the past few days. We should take advantage of such beautiful weather."

The argument seemed valid, and Leslie couldn't think of any better way to assure she wouldn't wind up in his arms again. "Fine," she said.

While he dressed, Leslie sat down and reproached herself for coming apart in his arms. Yet she could not evade the feeling of walking through the looking glass, into a wonderland of danger and adventure, whenever she was in his presence. He wasn't for her, she reminded herself. He was everything she did not want in a man, and she would not let herself get attached to him. It was just the atmosphere he created, the unreal way he kept appearing in her life, the sensual way he had met her today, galloping onto the scene and declaring himself a suitor, wearing a pair of cutoff jeans instead of a suit of armor, challenging the man who considered her his own. Things would settle down when he was dressed and they were out under the bright sunshine, she assured herself.

But when he came out of the bedroom tucking his T-shirt into his shorts, her assurance fled. He was just as magnetic in clothes as he was out of them.

He reached for the camera bag sitting on the counter and hung it around his neck. "You never know when I might want to remember something," he said with a teasing grin.

Grabbing his payroll books and files Leslie had brought, he led her out onto the redwood sundeck, which was furnished with several redwood chairs and a picnic table beneath an umbrella. She watched him as he settled across from her at the table, opening one of the files. She watched the play of light on his face as he concentrated on the work in front of him, and the vulnerable hint of seriousness that seemed so far away when he grinned and flashed that dimple. She wondered how his mind worked, what pattern he followed. Everyone had a pattern, didn't they? But so far, his remained undefined. Every time she thought she had him pegged, he surprised her.

He was a puzzle, and she feared the working of the puzzle would be her undoing.

Leslie's mind couldn't have been further from tax tables and government forms as she watched Scott shuffle through the pages. He fit perfectly into his surroundings, she thought, letting her eyes drift to the green and wooded expanse of property.

He looked up at her, caught her inhaling the fresh morning scent of grass and wind. He smiled. "Nice, isn't it?"

"It's beautiful, Scott," she admitted. "Is all this land yours?"

"All mine," he said. "One day I'm going to build a huge house right smack in the middle of it. And I'll just fish and ride horses and take pictures all day long."

Trying to conjure up the image, Leslie closed her eyes. Opening them again, she asked, "Is that what you do now? Just take pictures and play all day?"

His expression hardened suddenly, and for a moment she feared she had hit a nerve. But then the hardness disappeared and his dimple reappeared. "What if I do?"

"I didn't mean anything by it," she said honestly. "But your show is only two hours every night."

"So what do I do all the rest of the time? Besides taking pictures?" He nodded toward the files. "I told you I own those businesses."

"I know, but..."

He smiled and propped a foot on the bench beneath him, setting an elbow on his knee. "No, you're right, I don't go in to an office every day. Just believe that I keep busy. And my photography is pretty important to me. Besides, a lot more work goes into being Nick Nemoy than you know."

She traced a knot in the grain of the table. "Like what?"

"Like research. I can't argue about politics and foreign policy and what's happening up the street if I haven't done my homework. I read a lot and I study a lot. I have to know both sides of every argument, because I always take the opposite side of the caller."

His admission amazed her. "Even when you know you're wrong?"

"It isn't a question of being right or wrong," he said. "It's a question of stimulating an intelligent discussion."

"Telling a man to stick his head in the oven is an intelligent discussion?"

He laughed. "I get a lot of crackpots calling in, and I try to discourage them."

"But you discourage everyone who calls in. You insult them needlessly."

"They still call."

Leslie shook her head. It was useless. He would not be convinced he was doing anything wrong. Propping her chin on the heel of her hand, she studied him, determined to figure him out. "I can't believe it. You seem like such a decent person, and then every night you turn into some kind of ogre. It doesn't fit you, and I have a lot of trouble believing you aren't just a

tiny bit schizophrenic. Nothing about Nick Nemoy is
consistent with Scott Jenkins.''

Scott dropped his leg and stood up, opening his
camera case as he spoke. ''Les, Nick Nemoy *is* Scott
Jenkins. And everything about me is consistent. You
just don't want to see it. I believe in my show. I believe that I'm making a lot of people in this city think
about things they ordinarily never would have.''

''Who cares whether they think about those things?
Why does it matter?''

Scott's face became tight and tired. He set down the
camera and leaned onto the table facing her. ''It
matters when most of our citizens don't know who the
secretary of state is, or what countries we're giving
military aid to, or what countries are starving. It
matters when they turn their backs on cold-war issues. And it matters even more when they're apa-
thetic about what happens at their own child's school
or to the neighbor across the street. I want to make
them think, form opinions about those things. So I
make outrageous statements about the issues and take
ridiculous stands, and they fight with me. And the
ones who listen and don't call in sit out there and get
angry and upset. But before the show's over, they believe something. Maybe it's not what I want them to
believe, or what I believe. But don't you see? They
believe *something*.''

Leslie sighed. If only he was acting out of igno-
rance. If only he didn't know better. ''What good does

it do society to tell a woman complaining about her marriage to divorce her husband?''

Scott's expression softened when he realized she was referring to her mother. He stood up, propped a foot on the bench and leaned forward. "Les, sometimes when a person is angry or depressed and considering taking action, it helps to suggest that action. Sometimes it slaps them in the face and they think harder about it.''

"My mother didn't think harder about it. She left my father.''

"She just took a little vacation that she, no doubt, needed." He straightened and picked up the camera again. "But as they say, 'The opera's not over till the fat lady sings.' ''

Leslie narrowed her eyes and cocked her head. "Is that supposed to mean something?''

He shrugged. "Just wait. In this state she can't get divorced until a year after separation. A lot can happen in a year.''

"How do you know all that? Are you divorced?''

He raised the camera to his face. "Nope. I used to be a lawyer.''

Leslie caught her breath and opened her mouth as she saw yet another piece in his puzzle, a piece that sparked even more questions. "You what?''

He smiled and snapped a picture, which only added to Leslie's frustration. Before she could protest and ask him to repeat himself, he was standing up, snapping pictures of her as if afraid he'd miss that one expression worth remembering.

CHAPTER FIVE

"Did you say you were a lawyer?" Leslie asked as Scott hid behind his camera, moving left and right, forward and back, snapping pictures of her with the wind behind her, blowing her hair in wisps that she pushed behind her ears. Her frowning face held disbelief and curiosity, and the fact that he was recording her expression did not make her alter it. "A real attorney?"

He nodded. "Once. Oh, that's nice. Lean your head like that again."

She looked away. "No. I'm not a model. Why aren't you a lawyer anymore? Did you get disbarred?"

He lowered the camera from his face and sent her a punishing glance. "No, I was not disbarred. I resigned from the bar. I had a very busy, very lucrative practice, and I gave it up." He raised the camera again. "This is great. Your surprised look is priceless."

"Stop doing that!" she shouted, pushing back her chair. She stood up and moved to the rail of the sundeck. "You're making me nervous. I want to know why you gave up your practice. What kind of lawyer were you?"

He squatted and brought the camera down, a hint of annoyance in his eyes. "I was a criminal defense attorney."

She seated herself on the wooden rail, relieved that his camera was no longer aimed at her. "Were you good?" She knew he'd say yes, and she expected an arrogant grin, would welcome it.

But he surprised her. Unsmiling, he raised the camera to his face again and refocused the lens. "Too good."

The frustration was evident on Leslie's face—frustration mixed with the need to understand. "What do you mean?"

He didn't answer.

"Please, I'd really like to know."

He brought the camera down to just below his eyes, and she saw a pleasant sparkle in their dark depths. "You want to know about me, Les?" he asked.

She swallowed and lowered her gaze, and the camera clicked. "Yes. I really do." The admission came as a surprise to her.

He got his camera case off the table and moved closer to her, leaning a hip against the rail she sat on. His face was sober, quiet, contemplative. He studied his camera, pulled another lens from his case, replaced the one he'd been using. "I was a good attorney," he said as his fingers fumbled with his camera. "So good that very few of the people I defended had to pay for their crimes."

"You defended people who were guilty?"

He shrugged and looked at her. "It was my job, Les. But you have every right to be appalled. The only thing that kept me at it was that there *were* some—many—who were innocent. But sometimes I wasn't sure, and I defended them anyway. And usually just before the trial was over, or after my client was freed, I'd learn for sure that I'd defended a guilty man." He raised his camera and captured the look of renewed disenchantment on her face.

Did the horrible surprises about this man never stop, Leslie wondered. Each time she asked a question, she hoped he would say something that would change her opinion and make it all right to be entranced with him. But each answer provided nothing more than another reason for her to stay away.

"It got to me, too," he offered softly. "I didn't like myself very much, but I kept thinking I'd spent so many years getting where I was that I couldn't just throw it all away."

"Why didn't you become another type of lawyer?"

"I got bored easily. Corporate law wasn't for me, and I didn't want to get stuck handling divorces and small lawsuits of no real significance. I liked the excitement of criminal law, but sometimes I didn't like the consequences. Hell, the other side was just as bad. The district attorney dirtied his hands with plea bargaining and making deals. He helped as many of them go back on the streets as I did."

Leslie dropped her eyes and traced her palm with a forefinger. She remembered the sarcastic clipped voice of Nick Nemoy and the arrogant way he'd looked when she'd caught him at his profession—leaning back in his chair with his feet propped up and a smug expression on his face. Was that how he'd been as a lawyer? The camera clicked again, and he brought it down and looked at it, his face pensive.

"My disillusionment built up gradually. A few times I thought I'd go crazy. If the ridiculous maddening pace didn't kill me, I figured my conscience would. The last straw came when one of the clients I'd proved innocent went out and killed again." His voice broke and he paused, clearing his throat. He raised his head and turned his face into the wind.

As Leslie watched him, she saw moisture gathering in the corners of his eyes. His grief at the memory made her own eyes well. She wet her lips and reached for his hand, but he only raised the camera again and snapped her picture. Used to the picture taking by now, she hardly noticed. "Is that when you quit?"

He nodded and continued pressing the shutter, faster, as if filling a need to bury himself in another subject. "I had these businesses and some other investments then, and I lived off them and my photography for a while. And I had a pretty hefty bank account. I haven't regretted my resignation for a second."

She watched him for a long moment, staring directly into the camera as if she could see through it to his face. Was that what she'd wanted to hear? That he'd got out? That he'd changed? Or that he'd never *had* to change from the man who couldn't fit into the mold the justice system had created for him? "How did you become Nick Nemoy?" she asked, hoping to rid him of the solemnity the memory of his last client had brought.

He lowered the camera and busied himself changing film. "I was pretty bitter after all that, and there was this guy who used to have a talk show much like mine—except he wasn't quite as obnoxious." A grin broke out over his face, providing such relief from the tension that Leslie couldn't help returning it. "His name was Willis Harvey. Do you remember him?"

"Vaguely," Leslie said, recalling coming across his evening show a few times and changing the station out of boredom.

"Well, I used to listen to his show every night. One night someone called in and started a tirade in defense of the justice system. So, being the natural-born debater that I am, I called in and stated my opinions on the subject." He laughed. "You think my show's obnoxious now. I was mad then. I can't even believe some of the things I said to Willis about that caller that night. Anyway, I started phoning every night, disagreeing with earlier callers and arguing with Willis. Willis talked about me when I didn't call, asking on the air where I was. I told him my name was Nick, and people started calling and asking if they could speak to me. It was really very funny. The station loved it, because it brought the ratings way up." He focused the camera again at Leslie's shaking head and snapped a picture. "To make a long story short, when Willis retired, the station asked me to take over his show." He spread his arms and shrugged.

"And that's how you became Nick Nemoy," Leslie said. "I can't believe it."

"Believe it," he said. "It's one of the best things that ever happened to me. I love what I do and I feel good about it."

Instead of inspiration, his words provided more discouragement. Not only did she feel as if she were cheating on Stephen every time she was near Scott, but the shadow of Nick Nemoy behind him proved that her interest would have been futile even if Stephen were not in the picture. Why was it so disheartening to know they could never be compatible? "How do you sleep at night?" she asked, not coldly, but in a way that begged him to make her understand.

The dimple again bit into Scott's cheek, and mischief sparkled in his eyes. He inched closer to her, until their shoulders touched. "Lately I have been having trouble," he rumbled.

Leslie could feel the warmth of his breath, more compelling and intimate than the breeze that blew her hair into her face. "Then your conscience does get to you?"

"Not my conscience. My imagination." His hand cupped her neck under her hair. "Every time I close my eyes I see a sassy little thing with green eyes and beautiful brown hair that makes a man want to bury himself in it." His hand molded itself to her shoulder and slid down her arm. "And a body that won't quit, no matter what covers it."

She sat up rigidly and straightened her shirt, an undeniable thrill coursing through her, making her shiver. "We really should get to work," she said, pushing herself off the rail.

He groaned and put out a hand to restrain her. "Just because I have a few harmless little fantasies?"

Leslie took a deep breath, her eyes on the files spread out on the nearby table. Refusing to give in to the attraction she felt, she forced all emotion from her face and looked at him. The sun, directly overhead now, made his hair look as soft and smooth as honey and his eyes as black as an abyss threatening to draw her in and never let her out. "As long as they remain fantasies, I suppose they're harmless. But if you don't mind, I'd rather not hear about them."

Leaning close, he whispered, "Come on, Les. Don't tell me a woman like you doesn't have a fantasy now and then."

She swallowed and tried to hide the trembling in her hands. "My fantasies aren't like yours, Scott," she replied in a shaky voice.

He leaned back again and studied her. "Tell me about them. Tell me about that knight in shining armor who's going to ride into your life representing all that's good, fighting all that's evil. Do you consider Stephen to be that knight?"

Leslie smiled. "Maybe. What's wrong with that?"

"Nothing's wrong with it," he said, reaching out to cup her chin and trace her lips with his thumb. "It's just that knights in shining armor are sometimes a little boring." He shook his head slowly, then spoke, enchanting her with his soft voice and intriguing words. "No, Leslie. A knight in shining armor is not for you. You need a man with a little spice. A little character."

"Someone like you, for instance?" she asked with the hint of a smile as he moved closer to her.

"Someone exactly like me," he said in a husky whisper. He pushed the hair out of her face, and her skin tingled where his fingers grazed her cheek. "Someone who knows what to do with a woman like you. Knights in shining armor have too many other things to think about. All those dragons to fight, all those battles to win. While guys like me, well, we have all the time in the world for concentrating on our women."

Leslie's gaze dropped to his lips, which were moving toward hers. She wet her own. "I'll bet you do," she whispered, trying to sound sarcastic and unconvinced, but her quavering voice gave her away.

Leslie's last shreds of restraint were stripped away as Scott's lips met hers. The kiss was hungry, probing, proving the words he'd just spoken. His arms closed around her, pulling her off balance, but he supported her suddenly fluid body with arms as steady and as strong as steel. His hands moved up and down the contours of her slender back, around her sides, dangerously close to her breasts. Leslie knew that another few seconds in his embrace would mean no turning back, for her control had vanished and her pounding heart had freed the reins on her impassioned spirit. She could not make herself stop the gentle circular motion of his hands, the havoc he was creating in her body.

The leaves and the breeze and the birds conspired with Scott, their gentle sounds harmonizing in a chorus that seemed bent on keeping her in this hypnotic state. Scott's questing mouth provided a distraction from his bold hands, and Leslie's own fingers explored the rippling muscles of his back and the bristled skin of his face.

As his hands molded the soft curves of her waist, his mouth opened and closed on hers, making her gasp with need, creating an appetite she'd never known existed. The intensity of her need frightened her, and when his lips at last left hers to nibble along her throat, she breathed the word "No."

Pulling his face back, he looked at her. Her eyes were smoky, heavy-lidded, eloquent, telling him the opposite of what she had just said. He sighed raggedly, then bent his head and kissed her again. And just as she again felt her control slipping away, he tore himself apart from her, sat down and buried his face in his hands.

Slowly she sat down beside him.

He took a deep shaky breath and raised his face, his eyes filled with emotions she'd never encountered in a man before. "I must be crazy," he said.

She stared off into the trees, wishing she had not uttered the single word that had shattered the moment.

Gazing into her eyes, he took her hands in his, and she could feel his trembling. "I'm sorry," he said. "Here I was trying to prove how much I could affect you, and I find myself getting completely carried away."

"I was pretty carried away, too," she admitted in a whisper.

He smiled and lifted his hands to her face, his gaze so piercing she could almost feel his mark on her soul. Grasping her hand, he pressed it against his racing heart. "Try feeling a reaction like that through a coat of armor," he said.

She pulled her hand away and looked past him, trying to remind herself that she should be relieved things had not gone further. "I shouldn't be here," she said in a shaky voice. "Stephen trusted me until today." Until she had met Scott, she had trusted herself.

Scott brought her face back to his. "I didn't stop kissing you because of Stephen. If the time was right for me to make love to you, all the Stephens in the world wouldn't have stopped me. You might have said no, but I know you didn't mean it."

Genuinely confused by her own feelings, ones Scott seemed to read so clearly, she lowered her eyes.

"I stopped because I still don't meet your standards," he mumbled. "I'm Nick Nemoy, as well as Scott Jenkins, and you can't accept that with or without Stephen."

His verbalizing so accurately her thoughts made her more uneasy. Was it love for Stephen that made her hold back? Or just guilt? Or even worse, could it be fear of falling for the wrong man and not one more honorable? "Why do you keep doing this?" she asked. "Ever since I met you, you've been trying to turn me upside down."

He smiled sadly and pushed her hair behind her ear. "Because you aren't like anybody else. I need a woman like you in my life." After a moment, he stood up and walked to the edge of the deck. Leslie watched his shoulders moving with his heavy breath. She got up and followed him.

Stuffing her hands in her pockets, she stood next to him, not touching him, and looked out over the greens, golds and browns of the land that was as breathtaking as he. "I wish I could tell you that my commitment to Stephen doesn't matter. I wish I could tell you that your being Nick Nemoy doesn't matter. But they do. Both of those things matter a great deal."

"But I get the distinct impression that Stephen wouldn't matter quite so much if Nick Nemoy didn't exist."

Leslie couldn't answer. She wasn't certain and the uncertainty made her hate herself.

He looked up into the sky, crossed his arms, nodded his head. A long moment of silence followed. "Of all the people in the world who had to walk into my life at the exact time that lightning bolt was going to strike me, why did it have to be you?"

Leslie didn't answer and she didn't ask what he meant, for she knew. She had been struck with the same subtle yet powerful bolt of lightning, the silent flash of electricity that had fused their spirits together, no matter how unsuited they were for each other.

"Oh well," he said, going back to the table and sitting down. "I've been told my ego could stand a little bruising."

Leslie stepped toward him, wishing she could wipe the hurt from his face. "Scott, I'm—"

Holding up a hand to stop her words, he said sarcastically, "Don't. It's okay. Hell, I deserve it. A guy like me? Why should I expect to get involved with a woman of your standards?"

"That's not what I meant," she said, anxious for him to understand.

"It's okay. I mean, I haven't exactly come across as Mr. Perfect. Next thing you know you'll find out I pull the wings off flies and tie cats' tails together."

Leslie ground her teeth and crossed her arms. "Scott, you're exaggerating. I'm not judging you."

A dry laugh escaped through his taut lips, and he brushed a stiff hand through his hair. "Not judging? Well, thank you. I appreciate that. It must be hard to be so open-minded from where you stand."

Leslie stared at him for a long moment, watching his face take on the bitter expression of Nick Nemoy, just as his voice had already done. "Is that another comment about my ivory tower?"

Scott shrugged. "If the pedestal fits..."

Leslie swallowed the suffocating lump in her throat and turned away from the icy glaze in his eyes. "That wasn't fair." Her mouth closed in a tight line that, she knew, looked too much like a pout. "I think this was all a mistake. I think you should take me home."

He sighed with regret and looked down at the papers on the table. "We haven't gone over my books yet."

"Call Maggie," she said coldly. "She'll take care of your businesses for you. I never should have got involved."

Scott rubbed his temples, and his voice softened. "Les, I'm sorry. I didn't mean to be so hard on you. Come on. I need you to do my books."

Leslie swallowed, her throat dry. "Maggie is as capable as I am."

Scott's eyes were dark, apologetic. "Come on, Les. I don't want Maggie. I want you."

Raising her shoulders, she hugged herself as if the posture could keep her wits together. "Why? You seem to resent my principles, my values. Why don't you just leave me alone?''

In seconds Scott was off the chair, his firm hands closing around her shoulders. "I can't leave you alone," he said softly. "I don't seem to have a choice. And I don't *know* why. Maybe it's because you have such a distorted image of me. It keeps me on my toes. Makes me want to prove I'm better.''

"Is that what all this is about?" Leslie blurted. "You're just trying to prove something to me?''

He stepped back and dropped his hands. "No. I want you to like me. I want you to know that I'm not a cad. Believe me, Les, whatever I feel for you, it is definitely not resentment. You frustrate me to the point of madness, but I can't get you out of my mind.''

A tear dropped onto Leslie's cheek, and she batted it away. "Despite my ivory tower?''

He wiped the tear with the pad of his thumb and lifted her chin until her moist eyes met his. "Maybe that's part of what attracts me to you. I'll just have to make it my business to convince you you're wrong.''

Another tear escaped, but it fell on Scott's finger. "Don't cry," he whispered. "I don't have my camera ready.''

She felt a smile breaking through her whirlwind emotions, and she turned away from him, unwilling to let him see it. He reached for her and slid his arms around her waist, pulling her near. Expelling a long sigh, she felt her body relax into him. "I really don't want to like you," she said honestly.

"I know," he said, squeezing her more tightly against him. He kissed her hair. "I'll just have to change that, won't I?"

She sighed again. "I don't know if you can."

"Well, I'll give it one heck of a try," he whispered, lifting one of her hands and pressing a kiss into the palm, branding her there as he had already branded her soul. "Now come on. We have work to do."

Since the sun was getting too warm for comfort, they agreed to go inside to work on the books, an unspoken truce keeping them from yielding again to the chemistry sizzling between them. The afternoon was long and tense, as the two avoided touching while they worked, and avoided any personal conversation. Leslie found that his books for the quarter that had just ended were in terrible shape, and in the stack of papers he handed her as an afterthought, she found that the IRS had penalized him for overdue taxes. As if that weren't enough, his payrolls were a mess, for the social-security tax he'd withdrawn was lower than the current rate. To top matters off, his bookkeeping had been so haphazard that much of the time he switched debit and credit columns midmonth. The problems made her crazy, but confirmed his need for some sound bookkeeping.

By the time the sun was setting, Scott and Leslie were hungry and exhausted. "I think I've got enough to get started on," Leslie said, closing his books. "I may have bitten off more than I can chew here, but I can see you do need help." She stacked his payroll books on top of the files. "How have you kept up with these in the past?"

Scott shrugged and stood up, stretching his long limbs. "I did the best I could. The government penalized me a few times, but I don't really have enough work there to retain an accountant. Until I met you I had no idea there were businesses that did this kind of thing."

Leslie stood up. "That's why I started this," she said. "I used to work at an accounting firm, and a lot of our clients could only afford to come to us once a year to do their annual taxes. I could see they really needed help year-round." She took a breath and stretched. "Well, I'd better get going," she said finally. "It's late and I'm getting hungry."

"Sorry I took up your whole day off," he said, pushing her hair out of her face.

She smiled. "I enjoyed it."

"In spite of yourself?" he asked with a crooked grin.

She lowered her eyes and didn't reply. "I'll take the books and the files out to the Jeep."

Scott caught her arm as she started to leave. "Les, stay. Have dinner with me tonight. It's my night off."

The offer was tempting, but the thought of dealing with Stephen if she spent the evening after she had already spent the entire day with Scott was enough to make up her mind. "No, I can't. I really think we should stop seeing each other on a personal level. I mean it." Her voice was apologetic, and he nodded in solemn reluctant agreement.

"Well, I guess I can only hope you'll get hung up on my books and need another 'in-depth' discussion with me." He smiled, and the warm expression coaxed a similar response from her.

"I'll call if I need you," she said.

"May I call if I need you?"

Leslie thought for a moment, considering the many different ways she could interpret that question. "I guess so."

Smiling wryly, he placed his arm around her shoulders and led her to the Jeep.

CHAPTER SIX

"LOOKS LIKE OL' SNEEZY'S waiting to have it out," Scott said with a half grin when he pulled in behind Stephen's car, still parked in her driveway. "Want me to come inside with you?"

"No, thank you," Leslie said without hesitation. "I'll handle Stephen."

Shrugging in resignation, Scott wished her luck and drove away.

Leslie took a deep breath and went inside. Stephen was waiting in her office, a book in his lap, watching out the front window. "Short meeting," he said sarcastically.

"Have you been here all day?" she asked, setting down the stack of books and files she'd brought home.

"All six hours," he said. He had combed his hair, and his shirt was tucked in. She wondered if he had forgotten he had pneumonia. "Isn't that a bit long for a business meeting?"

"Not particularly," she answered, going into the kitchen and opening the refrigerator. "Not for a new client. That's why we planned it for a Saturday." She stared at the contents of the refrigerator. A six-pack of diet colas, a bag of carrots that had gone soft, two eggs. The emptiness there seemed to fill her, too, darkening and widening voids she'd never known she had.

Stephen stepped behind her, sliding his arms around her waist. "I'm sorry. I don't know what's got into me today. It must be the fever. Forgiven?"

The question made her angry. Didn't that man know he had every reason to be angry? Didn't he realize the fears he'd had that morning were well founded? Didn't he understand that she needed him to be strong if she was going to get through this infatuation unscathed? "Of course," she said, turning.

He cupped her face, but his hand against her skin felt cold and soft compared to Scott's. "I know you wouldn't do anything to mess up what we have," he said quietly. "You aren't the type." His arms closed around her, squeezing her tightly against him, but instead of feeling secure she felt more alone and more afraid. Stephen was afraid, too, she knew, but was handling it the best way he could. The wrong way.

"What type am I, Stephen?" she asked, pulling back to look at him.

"You're beautiful and reliable and honorable." His voice fell a degree. "And you're mine. I think that Jenkins fellow probably knows that by now."

Leslie breathed a sigh that held a sob behind it. Reliable, honorable. She knew she wasn't either of those things. She was a woman. One who could be swept off her feet. One who could fall in love when she didn't want to. One who could hurt a man who cared for her.

"Stephen," she began, trying to find a way to tell him she had betrayed him by kissing Scott—not once, but several times since she'd met him. But his trusting expression stopped her.

"That's enough about that idiotic fight this morning," he said, turning her back toward the refrigerator. "Why don't you just fix us something to eat and we'll sit down and watch a good movie on television? And could you fix me a hot toddy? My throat is pretty sore."

Leslie sighed. "I don't have any food, Stephen. And I'm tired. I was thinking of ordering a pizza."

He grimaced. "A pizza? Do you have any idea what Italian sauce and pepperoni would do to my throat?"

Leslie went to the couch and sank down without ceremony. "Then maybe you shouldn't eat. Aren't you supposed to feed a fever and starve a cold? Since you have both—"

"Don't be cruel, Leslie," he said petulantly. "It won't hurt you to make a bowl of soup for me. I've been sitting here waiting for you all day."

"No one asked you to, Stephen. If you were sick, you should have gone home and gone to bed. Do you want the pizza or not?"

"I want a little consideration," he snapped.

"So do I!" she shouted. The argument started a throbbing in her temples, an ache that crept to the base of her skull. Massaging the area, she wondered what was wrong with the pair of them. She and Stephen were worried that another man had come between them, so instead of getting to the root of the problem, they argued about pizza!

"Look," he said. "What's going on with you? You don't usually mind doing little things for me. If we were married—"

"We are not married," she bit out. "And if you come right down to it, we aren't really even engaged. If I want pizza I will order pizza."

"Fine, dammit," he said, his voice raising. "Order the pizza. Choke on it, if you want to. Get heartburn and eat alone. I don't know why I care!"

Leslie was forming a reply when the doorbell rang. Hot with unvented anger over everything *but* the pizza, she rushed to the door and swung it open.

Surrounded by suitcases was her mother, her dark hair in disarray and looking badly in need of a set, her face paler than Stephen's in the peaks of one of his illnesses.

"Mother! I thought you were in San Juan!"

As her cab drove away, Abbie Torrence picked up two of her suitcases and started in. "I don't really want to talk about it," she said, going straight into the living room where Stephen had collapsed on the couch in frustration. "And if you're sick tonight, Stephen, you're going to have to put up with some competition. I'm sicker than you are, no matter what you claim to have."

"Mom, what's wrong?" Leslie asked, bringing the remaining piece of luggage in and waving Stephen to be quiet when he started to defend himself.

"The fatal error," her mother moaned, falling onto the recliner. "I drank the water. Couldn't even make it onto the cruise ship, which by the way, made me nauseous from ten miles away. I spent two horrible days in a motel in San Juan and decided to come home this morning when I thought I could make it all the way."

Leslie couldn't help grinning. "Dad's going to be thrilled."

"Oh no, he's not," her mother corrected. "Your father is not going to find out. As far as he is to know, I'm on the ship this very moment, being wined and dined by handsome millionaires clammoring for the next dance."

Stephen couldn't sit still for that. "Isn't that a little childish, Mrs. Torrence? I mean, the whole fight was over the cruise, and you wound up being unable to take it anyway. Go home and apologize. Get it over with."

Abbie sat up straight in the recliner. "I might have expected that from you," she said with distaste. "You're just like him. Just like all of them."

For once in her life, Leslie understood what her mother was saying. It wasn't the cruise her parents were fighting about, any more than the pizza was the issue with her and Stephen.

"I consider that a compliment," Stephen riposted, chin held defiantly high.

"You would," Abbie mumbled. "Schmuck!"

Leslie bit back her grin and took the moment while Stephen gasped to intervene. "Mother, Stephen didn't deserve that," she said without conviction. "If you aren't telling dad you're home, what do you plan to do for the next two weeks?"

"Move in with you," she announced. "I'll sleep in the guest room. You won't even know I'm here."

Leslie's face fell and her eyes drifted to Stephen. He smiled as if she'd got her just deserts. "Here?" she said, her voice unusually high.

"Where else?" her mother demanded. "I can't go home and let him fling I-told-you-so's at me for the rest of my life. Besides, I went away to reevaluate my marriage, and I still intend to do so."

"Mom, I can't hide you here. I never know when dad's planning to pop in."

"If he comes I'll just stay in the bedroom. Leslie, I housed you for eighteen years. The least you can do is put me up for two lousy weeks."

Leslie laughed, knowing that if she didn't give in to her mother now Abbie would go into a recitation of the nine long months she had carried her daughter, and the horrible first year during which Leslie did not once sleep through the night. "Of course you can stay, mom. It's just that I want you and dad to get back together. He needs you."

"All that man needs is a sheet of sandpaper and a piece of wood. I'm tired of being bored, Leslie. I'm tired of playing second fiddle to a bunch of cabinets." Abbie swallowed and took a deep ragged breath. "I feel terrible. I'm going to lie down," she said, rising, picking up one of her bags and heading for the guest room.

Leslie glanced at Stephen, who leaned his head back on the sofa and stared at the ceiling. "So, what are you going to cook?" he asked. "Obviously, your mother can't eat pizza."

Leslie walked over to Stephen and took his hand. "You don't look very well, Stephen. I really think you should go home and get some rest. You feel pretty hot. How are those chest pains?"

"Bad," he said, suddenly more interested in his lungs than his stomach. "I'll probably go have a chest X ray tomorrow. You can't be too careful with these things. I read about a man who thought he had bron- chitis and found out—"

"Don't talk," she said, pulling him up and steering him toward the door. "You're losing your voice." She gathered his books off the coffee table and handed them to him. "Now go home and get right into bed, and let me know what that X ray shows tomorrow, okay?"

Nodding acquiescence, Stephen shuffled out of the house.

"Drink plenty of liquids, too, all right? Talk to you tomorrow." Closing the door, she collapsed against it, hating herself for wanting to pack a bag and go as far as the next train would take her. How had life become so complicated? Why did it have to be such a head- ache?

Her problems were all rooted in one thing, she thought. Scott Jenkins. He had been the catalyst that had made her mother take drastic action. He had been the barrier that had sprung up to make her doubt her feelings for Stephen. Darn the man, she thought suddenly with a rush of loneliness. How had he managed to play such a part in all of their lives when they'd least expected it? How had he managed to take her heart when she thought she had given it to someone else?

Walking into her office, she looked out the window and wondered what he was doing now. Was he thinking of her, or were all those things he'd said today simply a part of his game? For the life of her, she did not know.

And for the life of her, she wanted to.

It was ten o'clock before her mother was finally settled in bed. Leslie had tried several times to get her to rest, but each time, Abbie would recall something else about her husband that drove her crazy and begin a new tirade.

When the house was quiet once again, Leslie dressed for bed and climbed under the sheets, wishing for the serenity of sleep to take her from her doubts and fears and depression. When the telephone beside her bed rang, she considered not answering it. But the possibility of the ring's waking her mother was enough to change her mind.

"Hi, beautiful," Scott's lazy baritone rumbled.

"Scott," she said, an unconscious smile curving her mouth.

"I know we said we'd keep things on a business level, but if you remember, you said I could call if I needed you." The soft sound of his voice sent shivers down her spine. His next words sent a strange heat through her midsection. "I need you now."

"What for?" she said in the same soft tone.

"I've kind of grown attached to you," he said. "I needed to hear your voice. I was lonely."

"You? Scott Jenkins?"

He laughed lightly. "Yeah, me. I was just sitting here asking myself why I didn't call any of those women in my little black book...."

"You have a little black book?" she asked on a laugh, though the thought of competition was unsettling.

"Yeah," he said. "But my interest in those names seems to be waning. So I called you."

Leslie pulled the pillow out from under her head and hugged it against her chest.

"Les?"

"Hmmm?"

"I wish you could see me as I really am. We could be so good together."

The sudden dryness in her throat prevented Leslie from speaking. Yet what could she say? All she really wanted to do was tell him to come over and hold her and make it all right for her to love him. But she knew she mustn't. Too much was at stake. After a few days, a week, she'd have a rude awakening, and she'd see how wrong she'd been to follow her emotions.

"I'm sorry," he said. "Guess I'm out of line."

"No," she said, suddenly afraid he'd hang up. "Don't be sorry. You make me feel...special."

"You are special."

She sighed. "You also confuse me."

"Good," he said. "Maybe that's a promising sign."

Idly her finger traced the circle of the receiver, wishing she could feel his lips, which sounded so close to the phone.

"Did Sneezy finally leave?"

Leslie closed her eyes and smiled. "Yes, Stephen left."

"Can I come over?" he asked quietly.

She swallowed. "No. That wouldn't be a good idea."

She heard him sigh and longed for the feel, the taste of his mouth. "Okay," he said finally. "When can I see you?"

"I don't know. Maybe we should just play it by ear." The suggestion surprised her, for she had never played anything by ear in her life. But the idea of telling him they couldn't see each other at all shook her more than she wanted to admit.

"Okay," he said, and she could hear a pleased note in his voice. "I'm going to believe that means I'm breaking you down."

She smiled again. "It means you caught me in a weak moment when I'm too tired to think rationally."

"Sounds intriguing. Are you sure I can't come over?"

"Positive."

"Well then, I guess I'll let you go. Les?" he asked, before she had the chance to say goodbye.

"Yes?"

"I intend to dream about you tonight."

A warmth that Leslie was beginning to get used to when thinking of him spread from her core to her fingertips. "Bye," she whispered, and hung up the phone.

She continued to cling to the pillow as if it were a warm body, and her dreams of Scott began even before she slept.

CHAPTER SEVEN

LESLIE'S DREAMS OF SCOTT did not cease with the passing of a week, and his phone calls late at night only served to remind her where her heart really lay. Although recovered, Stephen stayed away. He was busy with a research paper, he said, but Leslie knew his absence was principally because her mother's outspokenness where he was concerned made him uncomfortable.

"I don't know what you see in that man," Abbie said on Saturday afternoon as they sat eating the enormous lunch she had insisted on cooking. "Being the wife of a doctor will be worse than what I've had to put up with. You think he's busy a lot now? You wait until he has patients calling him at all hours of the night. There won't be any vacations or holidays...."

Leslie's mind drifted as her mother rambled on. She sipped her orange juice and wondered what life with Scott would be like. She had always considered Stephen's hectic schedule a blessing, for it gave her enough time and freedom to lead her own life. But Scott was another story. Any woman who committed herself to him would hate the times he wasn't around, the way she had hated each day since she'd last seen him a week earlier. He was a man who got under the skin, and she suspected that making love to him could become habit-forming. Each time he kissed her, she had felt herself drawn deeper under his spell. If those kisses had haunted her thoughts day and night, how would she function if things went further?

"It's your life, though," her mother was saying. "None of my business."

"What's none of your business?" Leslie asked absently.

"Your relationship with that man."

"Scott?" she said without thinking.

"Who?"

The slip brought Leslie back to the conversation. "I meant Stephen."

Abbie shrugged and pulled the society section out of the newspaper.

Suddenly, a loud knock intruded on the peace and Leslie jumped.

"It's the back door," Abbie said, jumping up and taking her plate and silverware to the refrigerator where she stashed them. "It must be your father! I'll hide in the guest bedroom. Not a word, understand? I'm still on that cruise."

Giving her mother a chance to get to her room, Leslie opened the door.

Her father stormed in. "What the hell is this?" he bellowed, handing her a postcard.

Leslie took it and looked down, saw her mother's scrawl about the wonderful time she was having and the mention of her stay in Curaçao. She wondered when she had mailed it. "Looks like a card from mom."

"Where is she?" he asked, looking around the room for a clue.

"Says here she's in Curaçao," Leslie said, bracing herself, since it was obvious from her father's rage that he knew something was amiss.

"Look at the postmark!" he shouted. "It's postmarked New Orleans. That woman isn't on any cruise. Where is she?"

Leslie sighed. "Dad, I don't know. Maybe it's a mistake. Maybe—"

Her father raised a finger and shook it in her face. "When you see her you tell her I'm on to her. Tell her I know what she's up to."

So that her father wouldn't see her look of guilt, Leslie cleared her plate from the table and put it into the sink. "Dad, what on earth would she be up to? Whether she went on the cruise or not, she still left you. Anger isn't going to save your marriage at this point."

"No, but telling her off might save my sanity. That woman is driving me crazy!" He opened the door and started out. "You warn her for me."

Leslie collapsed into her chair when her father slammed out of the house, and after a few minutes when she was sure he had left, Abbie emerged. "Lowdown, good-for-nothing..."

"Mother, how could you?" Leslie asked wearily.

"How could I what?"

"How could you send a postcard to dad from here? He isn't stupid."

Abbie threw up her hands in self-disgust. "I haven't been thinking clearly lately. The postmark never occurred to me." Covering her mouth with both hands, she looked at Leslie with dread-filled eyes. "Oh, no. That was just the first one. I mailed another one yesterday. He's going to get another one postmarked New Orleans."

Leslie nodded slowly, pursing her lips to keep from making a comment she would regret. "Well," she said finally, "at least we know to expect dad to storm in here Monday. This time it won't be a surprise." Her eyes softened, and she took her mother's hand. "Mom, please go back to him. There's no use putting it off. He knows you're in town."

"I will do no such thing. I will stay here until I feel that he is calmer and more willing to listen to me." She slapped her thighs. "Besides, I've been making myself useful. Have you seen your office this morning?" An anxious glint sparkled in her mother's eye.

"No, why?" Leslie asked with a note of dread.

"I straightened it up for you. That stack of files you had behind your desk? I filed every one of them. Cleaned your desk off, too, and got rid of all those little receipts that were cluttering up everything."

"Mother, you didn't!" Leslie shouted, rushing for her office. "Oh, no. Oh, no," she wailed when she saw what Abbie had done. "Those little receipts were totals I've been working on for a week. And those files were the ones I hadn't worked on yet. I don't file them until *after* I've finished with them. Now they're all mixed up and I won't know what's what! Oh, how could you?"

Abbie's proud face fell and tears welled in her eyes. "I just thought I was helping. You seem so busy that you don't have time to get everything done. I just assumed—" A sob cut off her voice, and she went to the file cabinet and opened it. "I'll try to remember which ones I—"

Leslie caught her mother's hands and pulled them back. "No, mother. Maggie and I will have to do it. It's okay. It won't take that long to correct the problem," she said. *No longer than three or four days,* she screamed inwardly. "It's no big deal. Don't cry."

At that moment the telephone rang. Leslie jerked up the receiver. "Hello!" she said gruffly.

"Leslie," Stephen said in his hoarse voice.

"Stephen, I'm in the middle of something," she said, cutting him off. "I'll have to call you back."

"But, Leslie—"

"Not now, Stephen," she shouted, and hung up the phone.

Her tears under control, Abbie found a tissue and blew her nose. "I'm sorry, honey. I come here to get my life straightened out and I wind up messing up yours. You've been real short with Stephen lately, and I know it's because I've frayed your nerves."

Leslie sat on the edge of the desk. "Mom, you have nothing to do with what's been going on with Stephen and me. That I can promise you."

"I'm okay now," Abbie said, leaving the office. "I promise not to step foot in your office again. Go ahead. Call Stephen back."

Leslie stared at the phone, wondering how long she could put off calling him. If only she could have a brief reprieve, a moment's peace.

The doorbell rang. The next round, Leslie thought, and wondered what disaster would befall her now.

But after the harried events of the morning, the sight of Scott in his cutoff jeans and a white pullover shirt that provided a distinct contrast to his tanned arms, was far from disastrous. In his hand was a single pink rose. He handed it to her. "For you," he said, smiling. "I'd tell you to be careful of the thorns, but you always are."

"It's pretty," she said, touching the velvety petals to her lips and inhaling the sweet fragrance.

"Thanks. I picked it from your garden."

Leslie shook her head and grinned up at him. "I should have known. So, what brings you here?"

"I wanted you to go somewhere with me," he said, leaning against the doorjamb. She had not yet let him in, for she couldn't bear the thought of having to explain who he was to her mother.

"Scott, you should have called first."

"If I'd called first you would have said no."

"Probably," Leslie said with a smile. "You wouldn't believe the morning I've had. My father found out my mother was in town and came raging over here, and then my mother cleaned up my office and now everything's misplaced—"

Scott touched her lips with a finger, silencing her. "Let me take you away from all this," he whispered. "Ride to Biloxi with me today. We've both been working too hard. Let's just go off somewhere where there are no hassles."

The idea of going to the lovely coastal town was terribly tempting, but Leslie wasn't certain she had the courage to leave everything behind her and disappear with Scott. "I don't know. I was supposed to call Stephen...."

"Come on, Les," he coaxed. "Things are just going to get worse if you stay. Your nerves are shot. You need to get away." He smiled at her hesitation. "Go put your bikini on under your shorts. We'll be the first to break in the gulf this year."

Leslie's eyes danced. Did she really have a choice, she wondered. Had she had a choice since the first moment she met him? "I don't have a bikini," she said.

Scott grinned, his dimple a long cleft in his cheek. "Then go without. I will if you will," he challenged.

Leslie cleared her throat and stepped back. "My one-piece should do nicely," she told him, wishing she didn't sound quite so prim.

"Then you'll go?"

"Your timing is miraculous," she said. "Give me five minutes. Come on in. But I warn you, my mother is going to have questions."

"Good," Scott said, looking down the foyer for the woman he'd heard so much about—directly and indirectly. "I've got lots of answers."

"Hello," Abbie said, peeking into the hall. "I hope I'm not interrupting anything. I just wondered who was at the door."

Leslie swallowed the gigantic lump forming in her throat. "Mother, I'd like you to meet Scott Jenkins. Scott, this is Abbie Torrence."

Scott reached for her hand. "Mrs. Torrence," he said.

"Call me Abbie," her mother said, her hazel eyes wide. "Have you two known each other long?"

"Not long," Leslie jumped in before Scott could answer. "He's a new client of mine." Deciding not to go into a long explanation, she headed for her room. "I'll be ready in a minute, Scott. Make yourself comfortable."

Stripping off her clothes as fast as she could, Leslie pulled out a dark-green swimsuit with a back cut to below the waistline and the legs cut high to the same point. The front was low, and as she put it on, she decided to change to one less revealing.

Just as she began to slide the straps off her shoulders, her mother appeared in the doorway.

"Are you crazy?" Abbie hissed. Leslie winced, anticipating the lecture that was sure to follow.

"Yes, probably," she answered, peeling the suit off further.

"I mean, don't take that off! It's gorgeous. And he's gorgeous! Where have you been hiding him?"

A surprised smile curved Leslie's mouth. Pulling the swimsuit back into place, she reached for her shirt and put it on. "Then you approve?"

Her mother pursed her lips. "And all this time I worried about your involvement with Stephen."

"Mom, I'm still involved with Stephen. I just need to get away for a little while and breathe. Scott offered to take me to Biloxi, and I thought why not?"

Abbie sat on the bed as Leslie slipped her shorts back on. "My Leslie saying why not? I never thought I'd see the day. Now, let's see. If Stephen calls I'll tell him that you were called away on business and had to—"

"I'll deal with Stephen," Leslie said. "If he calls just tell him...tell him the truth. He won't like it, but I'll take care of it when I get back." Running a brush through her hair, she grabbed a towel and hurried back to Scott, her mother following close behind.

Scott was on the couch, absorbed in a photo album she kept beneath her television set. He looked up when he heard her.

"The photography leaves something to be desired, but the subject is intriguing," he said with a warm smile. He turned the page, and his smile turned to a smirk when he saw one of her and Stephen. Rolling his eyes, he closed the book and set it on the coffee table. "Ready?"

Leslie nodded and said goodbye to her mother, who followed them to the door, promising not to touch anything in her daughter's absence.

"I see you got your Mercedes back," Leslie said as she climbed into the car.

"Nothing but the best for my lady," he said, leaning in and dropping a kiss on her cheek before closing the door.

Leslie felt she should protest that she was not his lady, but the idea warmed her. She had no doubts that countless women would kill for the title and wondered how many had received it. But she was not countless women, she reminded herself. She was someone who knew what lay beneath the Scott Jenkins exterior. She was someone who had more scruples than to let her emotions rule. When the infatuation had played itself out, she told herself, she would go back to normal.

Conversation on the short drive to Biloxi, on the Mississippi coast, was casual and comfortable. Their discussion ranged from her parents' problems to Maggie's most recent fling. By the time they were cruising along the highway skirting the beach, Leslie had forgotten her earlier tension. Scott was telling her amusing stories about his brothers, and her laughter erased all traces of anxiety.

When he pulled over at last, it was into a small parking lot near an abandoned stretch of beach that was invisible from the highway. They got out, leaving their things in the car until they had decided on a good spot to station themselves. Holding hands, they walked to the water's edge, dodging the cool April waves as they frothed in over the sand.

"Wanna take a swim?" Scott asked, drawing her suspiciously close to the water.

She shook her head. "It's cold. Maybe after the sun has warmed it more."

"Oh, come on, Les," he said. "You really want to. Everyone has to indulge themselves now and then."

Leslie shook her head and backed away, but Scott moved with her.

"I'm giving you until the count of three, and then you go in with or without clothes," he warned. "One, two, three!" In seconds, his arms were around her and she let out a scream as he lifted her and ran with her into the cold waves. When he stood waist deep, he fell backward, pulling her underwater with him, the two of them laughing and flailing for breath as they surfaced in each other's arms.

"You're going to pay for that," she whispered through shivering lips, her arms clinging to his neck.

"Happy to," he said, raking his fingers through her wet hair, pulling it back from her face. Clothes clinging to their bodies, they drew even closer, their ragged breaths mingling. His eyes seemed darker when surrounded by wet spiked lashes.

Scott lowered his lips to hers, closing over them, sending a shiver through her body that had nothing to do with the cold. Suddenly he ended the kiss. Pulling away from her, he smiled and said, "I'll race you back to the car."

Together they took off running, falling in the sand and getting back up and running some more until they reached the car, breathless and exhilarated. "Okay. Let's get you out of those clothes," he said, opening the trunk.

Intoxicated with the pleasure of being with this seductive creature from a fairy-tale world where nothing made sense and logic had no place, Leslie laughed. "I've heard propositions before, but never one like that."

He peeked around the trunk, grinning as if about to burst into laughter. She wondered at the clarity and brilliance of his dark eyes when he looked at her, and for a moment, let herself believe that the world had been created for the sole purpose of bringing them together. "You'd better watch out, Les," he said, grabbing her hand and pulling her toward him. "Your rejections are getting less adamant. You don't get that indignant look on your face much anymore."

Leslie let him pull her arms around his wet waist, and she smiled up into his eyes, wondering if she should raise her guard or ride the tide of chemistry building between them. Her eyes were blazing emeralds. "Oh well. You were the one who said people should indulge themselves."

His grin faded and he asked, "Are we talking about my indulgences or yours?"

Leslie worried that she might be allowing herself to get into deeper water than she could manage. She tried to erase the look of longing from her face and cleared her throat. "I just mean I'm glad I came with you today."

"I'm glad you did, too," he said, still holding her. "I'm sorry you had a bad morning, but if it took that to make you run away with me for a day, I'm glad it happened. I've always said timing is everything." She shivered, and he laughed. "Cold?"

"Freezing," she replied. She pulled her shirt out of her shorts and wrung out the hem, creating a puddle on the pavement.

He slipped his own shirt off over his head. "Take your shirt and shorts off, Les," he coaxed gently. "They can dry in the sun."

Reluctantly Leslie stripped off her shirt, feeling naked despite the scanty swimsuit. She tried to ignore his eyes resting on her, as she handed the wet garment to him. He stood holding it, not turning away or discarding it. His eyes remained fastened on her as she peeled the shorts down over her hips and stepped out, knowing her breasts were straining visibly against her suit, knowing Scott could see the terror and exhilaration he aroused within her.

When she handed the shorts to him, he swallowed, took them from her and pulled out a large towel. Taking one last sweeping look at Leslie, he wrapped the towel around her, binding her arms. His face was inches from hers when he said, "Keep this around you

for now—at least until I get used to you—or I may not
be held responsible for my actions."

No man had ever made Leslie feel more desirable.
Stephen had told her occasionally that she was sexy or
beautiful, but the feelings those compliments had
evoked were nothing compared to what she felt now.
She wet her lips and wished they were not standing in
a parking lot in broad daylight within view of passing
traffic—wished there were some way to step into another dimension with him, where no one could interrupt or intrude, where no consequences had to be
paid.

They spread their wet clothing out on the hood of
the car to dry, gathered the blanket, extra towel and ice
chest Scott had brought and trekked back down to the
beach. When they had found a particularly well-
secluded spot, they laid down the blanket, and Leslie
sat on it with a sigh, feeling relaxed and peaceful as the
sun bathed her with its gentle heat.

Scott watched her turn over onto her stomach, and
she angled her head to see him as he stretched out on
his side. Setting his palm on her back, he began a
massage, his fingers moving sensuously in small, con-
centric circles. Leslie closed her eyes to hide the pleasure that glowed in their depths and rested her chin on
her folded arms.

"I wish I'd brought some tanning oil." He lowered
his face until his lips grazed her ear. "I'd love to rub
it all over you."

She felt her heart racing, and her practical side was thankful for the sound of traffic that went by on the highway above. The knowledge that they were not completely isolated was feeble assurance that things could not go too far.

His touch lightened, and he began to trace her spine with a fingertip. She felt her muscles tighten beneath his finger, not out of aversion to his touch, but rather as a means to control the impulse to discard her inhibitions and give in to the desire consuming her. When he withdrew his hand and flopped onto his back, she knew he had misread her reaction.

Though he was on his back, his face was turned toward hers, only inches away. Their eyes locked. "You're beautiful, Les," he whispered. "You know that, don't you?"

She swallowed and kept her head on her arms, unable to speak, almost unable to move.

His finger strayed to her chin, so close to his shoulder, and the touch was like a kiss. "I'm crazy about you," he whispered.

The slight forward movement of her head understated the lurch of her heart, and his fingers on her face guided her closer to him. As their lips met, his arms came around her, pressing her tighter into him, crushing her breasts, branding her with the soft imprint of the hair on his chest. Her hands learned the tightness of his bare skin and the soft places of his neck, then buried themselves in his hair. Oh, God, she

thought helplessly as the kiss grew deeper, more giving, more demanding. Did she love him already?

The kiss lingered on and on, and Scott gently turned
Leslie over until she lay beneath him on her back,
surrendering control to him. The magic and mystery
of desire swirling inside her seemed the natural beginning to an inevitable end. An end that would be its
own beginning. She wanted him. And though the
thought was still unsettling, she knew she loved him.

He broke the kiss slowly, his wet lips moving to the
corner of her mouth. His hands smoothed the hair out
of her face, and his dark eyes locked hers in the trap
she'd been trying to evade. *Love me without thought,*
they said. *Love me without condition.*

But the struggle in her own eyes spoke louder than
words.

Dropping a short kiss on her lips, Scott pulled himself up. "I think I'll go for another swim," he said.
"Wanna come?"

Leslie shook her head, then watched him as he
stalked across the sand to the edge of the water, his
strong dark figure silhouetted in the glaring sun. The
wind caressed his hair, the waves kissed his feet. He
stood pensively for a moment, kicking splashes in the
water, arms akimbo, gazing out over the horizon.

How could she tell Stephen, she wondered. How
could she tell him that two years meant nothing compared to the ten days she'd known Scott? And what
would happen if she surrendered to Scott? Would the
game be over, or would that just be the beginning?

But what if it's just an act? a voice inside her chanted. What if he was just good at making women surrender—even women like her who hated the Nick Nemoy side of him? She was certain he was quite the ladies' man, and how could he not be? He was easily the most handsome and charming man she'd ever met.

She sat up and wrapped her arms around her knees, her eyes following him into the cold water, watching him disappear into the briny waves, then emerge like Poseidon. She watched him wait for a high wave, then dive in, his deft virile arms splitting the water, taking him into the sea.

She was caught, she admitted at last, like a mortal child-woman, fascinated by the god who wooed her. Whether she liked it or not, she was in love. And she realized now that this was her first time. Everything she had felt for Stephen seemed superficial and meaningless now, in contrast to the dizzying passions that overtook her each time she beheld Scott Jenkins.

Her pulses jumped as she watched him emerge from the water. He stood facing her, the undulating waves bathing his feet as he ran his hands through his wet blond mane, shaking his head as if to clear it. At the sight of this man with the power to permeate her skin, steal her heart, she felt her every artery throb and her breaths become shorter and faster, as if her lungs had constricted. She hoped his swim was over, for she desperately wanted him near her again. She would ignore those nagging reservations today, she decided, and let herself forget all the reasons she shouldn't love him. Today she would allow herself that luxury, and nothing, she vowed, would spoil it.

When he reached the blanket, he grabbed a towel and dried off quickly. "The water's cold," he said, breathing heavily, "but it's nice. You should come in." Tiny beads of water webbed his golden lashes and glittered on the bronze curls of his chest.

She reached for his hand and pulled him down beside her. "I just want to sit here and enjoy the warmth for a while," she said softly. "It makes my problems seem a million miles away. I'll go for a swim later."

The afternoon flew by, and Leslie couldn't remember a time she'd ever enjoyed more. They sunbathed and played in the waves, then sunbathed and played some more. Finally they returned to the blanket after their last swim, ready to relax and get dry before leaving. As Leslie sat, Scott's eyes sparkled with the ghost of a smile, and he settled behind her, sliding his arms around her waist, pulling her back against him. She rested her head against his shoulder, felt him kissing the part in her hair, sending a shiver coursing through her. He leaned his cheek against her head and enclosed her hands in his, both pairs resting against her stomach while his thumbs caressed her wrists.

They sat like that for a long while. With body molded against body, they learned to know each other in silent blissful companionship.

When he finally spoke, the sun was beginning to set. Scott's voice was as soft and gentle as the dusk falling around them. "If I'm going to be in love with you, I need to know about Stephen."

"You don't have to worry about Stephen," she answered, not moving from her position.

His arms tightened around her waist. "Why?" He needed to hear it, but she wasn't sure she was ready to disclose her feelings yet.

"Because I'm not in love with him." *I'm in love with you,* she wanted to say, but the words were caught in her throat, her courage lost.

After a long quiet moment, he again spoke softly into her ear. "What are you going to do about him?" he asked.

"I don't know," she said. "I don't want to hurt him. He needs me. He believes in me."

"It's not just Stephen, is it?" Scott asked. "Am I my own worst enemy where you're concerned?"

Deciding not to break the bond of quiet loving companionship by being dishonest, she nodded her head. He pressed his face into her hair and squeezed her as if it might be the last time. "It's getting late," he said finally in a voice that revealed harnessed emotions. "Let's go home."

Their clothes were dry, and they dressed and loaded the car. When they drove away, he held her knee with his free hand, and she rested her hand over his.

The silence was broken when they reached New Orleans. With a somber expression, Scott glanced at her. His face was obscured by darkness, but she saw the worry eating at him. "Les, will you do something for me?"

"What?" *Anything,* her mind cried.

"Come to the radio station with me Monday night. Listen to me while I do my show. I want you to hear and see—understand—what I do."

The peace that had carried Leslie through the past few hours shattered like crystal. She didn't want to watch him at work. She wanted to forget Nick Nemoy so that she could continue loving Scott. "I can't," she said.

His grip on her knee tightened, emphasizing the urgency of his request. "Why can't you?"

She sighed, and her lip settled under her teeth. "I've heard your show," she said. "I don't like it. I'm trying to forget about it." Her honesty surprised her, but her words did not change Scott's tone.

"Les, my radio show won't go away."

She swallowed and moved her hand from his, but he caught and held it. "You haven't listened with an open mind. I want you to do that so you can see that in my own way I'm contributing something positive to society. I'm not perfect by a long shot, but I'm also not as bad a guy as you make me out to be."

"I know," she said. "It's just that it changes you. You're different when you're on the air." She paused, thought, tried to find the words to make him see. "I like you, Scott. In spite of everything I know about you. I just wish there wasn't that other side of you to complicate things."

This time it was Scott who removed his hand. "I'm not going to change," he said solemnly. "I like myself the way I am. And that's something that I haven't always been able to say."

By the time he pulled into her driveway, the air was thick with tension, smothering them like the dark blanket of night that now encased them. For a few long moments they sat in the car, neither making the move to get out. Finally, Scott slammed his hand on the steering wheel and shifted to face her. In a controlled voice that split the night, he asked, "What do you want from me, Les?"

"I don't know," she said. "What do you want from me?"

"A relationship," he said, moving his gaze to the dashboard. "One without Stephen. I want your trust." He looked at her, and she could see honesty lighting his face even in the darkness. "I'm lonely when I'm not with you, Les. And I've never felt that way about another woman. But just being with you is not enough. I want you to know and accept all of me. It's no good putting aside the things about me that you can't deal with and pretending they don't exist. And it's no good blaming your reservations about me on a relationship that obviously doesn't mean a lot to you."

"I know," she said, rubbing her eyes, only now realizing how tired she was. "But I can't help it. I don't like what you do."

He took her hand and pressed it to his face. "Just open your mind and come with me Monday night," he entreated. "Give me a chance." She lowered her eyes, and he cupped her chin, leaning his forehead against hers. "Just think about it," he pleaded. "I need you to understand."

"I'll think about it," she whispered, and her reward was a long gentle kiss that made her dread leaving him more than she'd dreaded anything in her life.

The bright glow of headlights on the street in front of her house jolted her back to reality. Turning around to see the car, she gasped.

Stephen had climbed out and was walking toward them.

CHAPTER EIGHT

BEFORE LESLIE HAD A CHANCE to speak, Scott had opened his car door and was getting out to meet Stephen in the yard.

Stephen's face was pale in the moonlight, a stark contrast to the sun-kissed color in Scott's. By the look on his face and the hard glint in his eyes, it was obvious he had seen Scott kissing her. "What the hell are you doing with her?" Stephen asked through gritted teeth.

"I'm bringing her home," Scott said, hands in pockets, his lithe body relaxed, yet appearing ready to pounce at the same time. "Not that it's any of your business."

"None of my business?" Stephen asked Scott incredulously. As an afterthought, he turned to Leslie. "None of my business?"

Leslie stepped between the two of them, a sinking feeling overwhelming her. "Let's talk about this inside." She started toward the door, but neither man followed her at first. It was as if they had made a challenge to each other, and Leslie braced herself and prayed that one of them—either of them—would have the sense to let it go. Finally, Scott turned his back on Stephen's glare and started toward the house.

Stephen stopped him. His hand slapped against Scott's sleeve, twisting the cloth. As quick as lightning, Scott wheeled around. His hand closed roughly on Stephen's collar, and in a voice so soft Leslie could barely hear it, he said, "Touch me like that again and I'll make you a case study for that medical school of yours. There's nothing I'd like more."

"Stop it," Leslie said. "Both of you. Come inside and we'll talk." She opened the door, letting the light from the house rob the front yard of its neutrality. Eyes shooting sparks, the two men dropped their hands and followed her inside.

Abbie was in the living room, and she stood up when the three entered. At the sight of Stephen she wilted. "Uh, excuse me," she said, hurrying out of the room. "I guess you all have some things to talk about."

Leslie stood in the center of her living room, both men's eyes trained on her, waiting for her to make a decision between them. She cleared her throat. "Stephen, I went to Biloxi with Scott today."

"Don't try to tell me it was business, Leslie," Stephen said. "I'm not stupid."

"No," she said. "It wasn't business." She looked at Scott, his dark eyes expecting so much, demanding so much. "I went because I wanted to."

"How long has this been going on?" Stephen asked, his nostrils flaring. "Have you been seeing him behind my back?"

"No," Leslie sighed, looking to Scott for help. "If today hadn't been such a spur-of-the-moment thing I would have told you before I left. I had every intention of telling you when I got back."

"What were you going to tell me?" Stephen snapped.

"That...that I wanted us to slow down a little. That..." Her voice faltered, and she swallowed. "Oh, Stephen. Don't do this. Don't make me stand here and tell you like this. I didn't want it this way."

"You wanted to break it to me easy?" Stephen asked, his eyes narrowing. "You wanted it to be clean and simple? Leslie, do you know who this guy is? Do you have any idea?"

"Yes," she said, uncertain of what he was leading to.

"I mean, do you really know who he is? Leslie, I did some checking today. This guy you've been seeing is Nick Nemoy!"

Scott stared at the floor. "She knows. I wouldn't let things go this far without letting her know that."

Stephen's face turned three shades redder. "Let things go how far?" he shouted. "Just how far have you gone with her?"

Leslie's body grew rigid. "Stephen! You have no right to make those kinds of assumptions."

"Why the hell not?" Stephen asked. "Doesn't two years give me any kinds of rights?" His voice softened, and he stepped toward Leslie, his hands held out to her to emphasize his words. "Leslie, don't let him do this. You've heard his show. It's all a game to him. See how many lives you can ruin in a day. See how many people you can turn into babbling idiots. Don't you see that his current game is fast-talking you into his bed?"

"You're out of line, Tate!" Scott fairly snarled. His broad chest heaving with anger, he turned to Leslie. "Don't listen to him, Les. You know better."

"Leslie, it's okay," Stephen said, setting his hands on her shoulders. "He's good at it. I understand how you can be taken in. But we can get over it. We can put it behind us. Whatever you've done with him, I forgive you."

Leslie backed away, pulling away from Stephen's hands. Her eyes were thick with tears, blurring her vision. "I don't need your forgiveness," she said.

Stephen took another step toward her, reaching for her shoulders again.

"Get your hands off her," Scott said in a steel voice.

"Shut up, Jenkins!" Stephen shouted. "You don't belong here. Why don't you get the message and just get out of here?"

"Not until Les tells me to," he said. "And if any messages have been handed out tonight, they were directed at you. I think you're the one who should leave!"

"You can both leave!" Leslie blurted.

The two men turned back to her, one with soft dark eyes with the potential to comfort and hurt at the same time, the other with cool gray eyes that saw, perhaps, the things she did not want to see. "Both of you," she said again. "Just go! I can't take this anymore."

Scott sighed heavily. "I think she's right. She needs to be alone."

"I'm not leaving," Stephen said flatly. "The very last thing she needs right now is to be alone. And I'm not taking the chance of your coming back here after I leave."

"He's not coming back tonight," Leslie assured him, wiping at the tears spilling down her face. "And neither are you."

"Leslie," Stephen warned, "I'm not going."

"Yes, you are, pal," Scott bit out, "if I have to drag you out myself."

Stephen ignored Scott's threat. Through his teeth, he said, "Leslie, if I leave here, there's no guarantee that I'll ever come back. I'm giving you the chance to change your mind. Don't be a fool."

"Get out!" Leslie said, storming past him and opening the front door. "Now." She leaned against the door, choking out sobs.

Slamming his hand into the jamb, Stephen went out. Scott hesitated next to her, touched her hand where it clutched the doorknob, then disappeared into the darkness. Leslie barely restrained herself from slamming the door, and walking back into the living room, tears rolling down her cheeks, she came face-to-face with an astonished-looking Abbie.

"Nick Nemoy?" the older woman asked, aghast.

"Nick Nemoy," Leslie answered, leaving her mother standing alone in the living room while she walked down the hall and closed herself in her bedroom.

MIDNIGHT. The glow-in-the-dark face of the clock seemed to have stopped there, never to move forward again. Leslie lay in bed and stared at it, wishing for relief from the depression that weighed on her. If she had not had such a wonderful day, the events of the evening might not have hit her so hard. *It's all a game to him.* Stephen's words echoed and reechoed in her mind, and she thought back over the days since she had met Scott. If it wasn't a game, why had he pursued her so unceasingly?

This was ridiculous, she thought. She had been with him today. She had seen his eyes, felt his hands, basked in his warmth. *If I'm going to be in love with you,* he had said when he'd asked about Stephen. And before Stephen had come on the scene, Scott had pleaded with her to try to understand. Her approval meant something to him. She *was* more than a game, wasn't she?

When the phone rang, she closed her hand over the receiver, praying it was Scott.

It was.

"Did I wake you, Sleeping Beauty?" he asked in husky intimate tones.

"Not really," she said, coming to a sitting position. "I couldn't sleep."

"Neither could I," he said. His mouth sounded close to the phone, and a slight shiver coursed down her neck as she imagined his breath on her ear. "I might be breaking the rules by calling you, but I was having these awful withdrawal pains, you know? And after tonight, I wasn't sure where I stood."

"After tonight," Leslie said with a weary exhalation of breath, "I'm not sure where *I* stand."

"It got to you, didn't it?" he asked quietly. "The things he said about me. You're wondering whether to believe them, aren't you?"

Leslie couldn't answer.

"Les, listen to me," he said. "What we had today was special. It could get more special. Please don't turn your back on me now."

Leslie sighed. She wanted more than anything in her life to believe him. "I guess I'm just wondering if anything can really be that special, or if I'm just floating through some kind of fairy tale that can't come true."

"I told you I wasn't a knight in shining armor," he whispered. "Since you found out I was Nick Nemoy, I haven't pretended to be anything I'm not."

Leslie smiled. "I know you're not a knight in shining armor. Which is one reason I have so much trouble figuring out why I'm attracted to you."

"So what if my armor's a little tarnished?" Scott asked, and she could hear the smile in his voice.

"My knight in tarnished armor," she whispered, running a finger in light circles across her pillow. "I think I like the sound of that."

A deep sigh whispered through the phone like a caress, alerting every nerve in Leslie's body. "I like the sound of it, too," he said. She heard the sheets rustling in his bed and imagined he was turning over. "Les, I know your mother's home, so I can't come to you. I want you to get out of bed and come over here tonight. I want to be with you."

An explosion of silence followed, the held breath of unconsummated lovers, more audible in its way than the heavy breathing they were capable of stimulating in each other. "You want me to come now?" she asked in a whisper.

"Yes."

She hesitated, then said, "I can't, Scott. Not yet."

"When?" he asked. "A week from Tuesday? May twenty-second? July ninth?"

She sighed. "I don't know when."

There was a brief silence followed by, "Dammit, Les, why can't you trust me?"

Leslie pulled her knees up to her chest and buried her face in them. "I do trust you. I do." The words were said from instinct, for her instincts told her to trust. But her mind warned her to remain guarded, to proceed with caution. "It's just so hard for me. Most of the people I know are either one way or another.

I'm not used to nonconformists. It's easy to trust a person who fits a mold. But you..."

"But I what?" he probed gently.

"You give off hard-to-read signals. Intellectually I'm wary of you."

"And emotionally?"

She swallowed, but knew the words needed to be said, before they erupted in some other way. It was safe here, on the telephone, she decided. "I'm falling in love with you." The words came out tremulously.

A moment of quiet added emphasis to the words.

"Are you afraid?" came the gentle question.

"Yes. I keep feeling like I need to reach out and grab something to stop my fall."

"Let yourself fall, Les," Scott murmured against the phone. "I promise I'll catch you. You won't be sorry."

She closed her eyes and remembered the strength in his. "I'll try," she whispered.

After a moment, he said, "I'll let you go now. I'll talk to you tomorrow, beautiful lady. And Les," he added softly, "I'm in love with you, too. Don't forget that. Good night."

The dial tone hummed its comforting message as she held the phone in her hand, smiling at the last words that had come through the receiver.

THE LAST MONDAY before the April fifteenth tax deadline was chaotic. Clients were in and out to confer about added deductions and tax breaks, and the telephone rang constantly with calls from clients who couldn't come in personally. Leslie and Maggie worked and reworked numbers until their eyes burned and their necks ached, and when Leslie had the chance to glance at the clock, she found that it was noon.

"No lunch today," she muttered to Maggie when, for the first time all morning, they were left alone in her office. "I haven't been to the grocery store, and I don't even have a loaf of bread. And there's no time to go out."

Maggie didn't look up from the forms scattered across her desk and, as if moving independently, her fingers made a rapid journey across the keyboard of her calculator. "It's okay. I'll cut up that cucumber in your refrigerator, and we can pretend they're cookies." She totaled her figures and looked up. "You know, people ought to lose weight for everything they don't eat. For instance, I could call and order a pizza right now, but if I don't, I should automatically lose three pounds, don't you think?"

"Sounds good," Leslie said absently, referring to the pizza. Just then the doorbell rang again. "Come in, it's open!" she shouted, as she had been doing all morning.

A delivery man carrying a couple of bags opened the door and stepped into the office. "Is there a Miss Torrence here?" he asked.

Leslie stood up, shrugging at Maggie who quirked her eyebrows questioningly. "I'm Leslie Torrence," she said, taking the bags he extended.

"I must be dreaming," Maggie said, slowly stepping around her desk to peek into one of them. "I
know I smell Chinese food."

"Compliments of Mr. Jenkins," the man said. "He
sent this note."

Leslie took the note, while Maggie took the food.
"Do you work for Scott?" she asked.

"Yes," the man said, offering a slight bow. "I'm
John Lee, a waiter at the Dragon."

Leslie held out a hand. "Well, it's very nice to meet
you, Mr. Lee."

The man bowed again and stepped back. "A pleasure meeting you, too. Now I must get back to the
lunch crowd. We are very busy this time of day."

"Of course," Leslie said. "And thank you for taking the time out to bring the food."

The man turned toward her at the door. "When Mr.
Jenkins has a request, we always carry it out. Enjoy
your lunch."

Leslie stood at the door and watched the man re-
turn to his car. She dropped her eyes to the note in her
hand, then glanced back at the bags of food, one of
which Maggie was already opening.

"What a guy," Maggie breathed. "What does the
note say?"

Leslie smiled and tore the envelope open. "'Dear
Les,'" she read aloud. "'I wanted to take you to lunch
today but knew you'd be too busy, so I did the next
best thing. Think of me while you stuff yourself.'"

Her voice trailed off when she came to the closing
message: *I love you.*

"Eat! Eat!" Maggie ordered, taking a mouthful.
"It's delicious."

Leslie took the other sack and unloaded it on her
desk, trying to concentrate on her work as she ate, but
only managing to think of Scott's big dark eyes, his
tanned arms around her, the warm clean taste of his
mouth and the sound of his voice when he'd said he
loved her. Her food grew cold as she stared dreamily
into space, but the sound of Maggie's laughter shook
her back to the present. She glanced up and saw Maggie's face, red with delight. In her hand waved a message from a fortune cookie.

"I think this was supposed to be yours," Maggie
said, thrusting the small strip of paper to Leslie.

Warily, Leslie read. "'Confucius say: a cold shower
only cures the symptom, not the disease.'" Maggie
collapsed in giggles, and Leslie felt her cheeks blush-
ing with embarrassment. Trying to suppress her smile,
she went to Maggie's desk where two other fortune
cookies lay. "I think maybe I'd better check those out
before you see them."

Maggie, still giggling, followed her back to her desk,
unwilling to miss out on the seductive messages. Reluctantly, Leslie opened the next one. "'You will meet
a tall, handsome, frustrated admirer at six o'clock tonight.'" Her eyes sparkled, and she smiled and handed
the note to Maggie.

She reached for the last cookie and pulled out the strip of paper. "'Fall and let me catch you. What's the worst that could happen?'" This one she folded in her hand, shaking her head when Maggie reached for it.

"It's that personal?" Maggie moaned.

Leslie nodded, a faraway look settling in her eyes as she wished for six o'clock. She had no choice but to fall, she realized. Nothing on earth was strong enough to break her descent now. But the last words nagged her. *What's the worst that could happen?*

A timid knock came on the door that led from the kitchen to the office, and Abbie, who had been told in no uncertain terms not to interfere with Leslie's work day for any reason, stuck her head in. "Honey, I hate to bother you," she said, "but can I talk to you for a minute?"

"No problem," said Leslie, and she went into the kitchen. Her mother was surrounded once again by packed suitcases. "Mom, where are you going?"

"I've been thinking about that other postcard I sent your father," she said. "He'll probably show up here any time now, and I'm really not up to facing him. I thought I'd find a hotel somewhere along the coast and spend a few days there. Then I'll be out of your hair, too."

"Mom, you're not in my hair," she said. "Don't go because you think I want you to."

"I really need a little more time before I have it out with your father," she said wearily. "I had hoped that by now something would have changed. But nothing has. He'll be ready to kill me by the time he finally catches me here.''

Leslie knew her mother was right. "Where will you go? When will you be back?"

Abbie shrugged. "Probably a Holiday Inn in Gulfport or Biloxi. And I won't be gone but a few days. Just long enough to decide what I'm going to do with my life next."

The sadness and hopelessness in her mother's voice pierced her heart. "Mother, please go back to him. He's angry now, but he'll come around. You love each other."

"That's not enough," her mother said dejectedly. "And since I'm the one who decided to leave, I'm the one who has to make some firm decisions. I've put up with him for too long. Even Nick Nemoy thinks so."

"Forget Nick Nemoy," Leslie clipped. "That's part of his act. He didn't know you when he gave you advice. You shouldn't have listened to him."

"Well, I did," her mother said. A horn sounded in the front drive, and Abbie picked up her suitcases. "That's my taxi. I'll see you in a couple of days."

As Leslie stood at the side door and watched her mother walk to the cab, an inescapable feeling of helplessness overwhelmed her. If only there was some way to convince her mother to go home.

When five o'clock rolled around, Leslie was still buried elbow-deep in paperwork. Maggie was loading her work into a carton to take home to finish. "The way I figure it," Leslie said blandly, "if we work around the clock every day this week we might get everything finished by the fifteenth. Remind me to give you a super bonus in your next paycheck.''

"Don't worry,'' Maggie said, blowing some long wisps of bangs out of her eyes. "I intend to write the check myself.''

The screen door at the back of the house slammed as someone came in, and Leslie rose from behind her desk to peer through the open door leading to the kitchen. "Who's there?''

"Me!'' her father yelled. "You hear that, Abbie? It's me and I'm on to you. I know you're here, so you'd better come out!''

Leslie rolled her eyes at Maggie and went into the kitchen. "Dad, she's not here.''

"Don't give me that,'' her father said with steely eyes. "I got another one of these intelligence-insulting postcards today. Go ahead. Tell her to come out and talk about this like a mature adult.''

"Dad, she was here, but she left this afternoon,'' Leslie said.

Sam's eyes narrowed and his face flushed red. "You mean to tell me she *was* here and you let her leave?''

"She knew you'd be coming over, so she decided to get out before you did.''

Maggie cleared her throat and picked up her carton of work. "Bye, Leslie,'' she almost whispered. "I'm going now.''

Leslie waved and turned back to her father, who was freshly showered and shaved. She wondered at the vulnerability in his eyes; it was the first time she'd ever seen it. He was a handsome man, she realized. His dark hair was combed to the side, and the etchings in his face added character instead of age. She saw what her mother had seen in him years ago, what had kept him attractive to her for nearly thirty years. "Dad," she said softly. "It's not too late to join her. You could try the Holiday Inns in Biloxi and Gulfport. By tomorrow you two could have all your problems worked out."

He cocked his head, running a callused hand along his stubborn jaw. "What kind of marriage did we have, anyway, when your mother just takes off like some flitty little teenager? That woman has never changed in all the years I've known her."

Leslie went to the refrigerator and got out a pitcher of lemonade. "Was mother a flitty little teenager when you met her?"

He shook his head, remembering. "You bet she was. Sassiest little thing I'd ever laid eyes on. Prettiest, too. Did as she pleased and nobody could stop her."

"Is that why you fell in love with her?"

Her father's face reddened, and she knew how difficult it was for him to share his feelings for his wife with his daughter. But the hint of a smile twinkled in his green eyes, the same emerald hue as Leslie's, as he gazed into the glass of lemonade she handed him. "No. It's more like I fell in love with her in spite of all that." He grinned without restraint. "Little rascal chased me till she caught me. Wouldn't take no for an answer."

Leslie dropped onto a stool across from her father. "I know the feeling," she said. She lowered her eyes to her father's hands, clutched so tightly around the glass that she feared he'd crush it. "Have you ever regretted it, dad? Marrying her, I mean."

He thought a moment, then slowly shook his head. "Not for a minute." Then he caught himself and straightened his posture, hardening his eyes and clearing his throat. "Not until she took off for that blasted cruise!"

Leslie grabbed his hand. "Dad, why can't you understand? She was trying to make a point. She's been neglected lately. You work too hard, and when you're home, you're not really home. She's been lonely. When you promised her that cruise, she was like a child-bride preparing for her honeymoon. And then you pulled out on her."

"Only because I had to!" he shouted, slamming his hand down on the counter top. "My best customer for twenty-eight years lost everything he owned in a fire. Now what was I supposed to do when he asked me to make his cabinets? Just tell him, 'No, I have to go take a cruise'? The man lost his home, and if I could give him back a little of it by making him the same cabinets I built him all those years ago, why was that so wrong?"

"It was wrong because he could have waited two more weeks. Obviously, your wife needed you more."

"Helluva way to show it!" he bellowed, standing up and almost knocking over his stool.

"You can still save your marriage!" Leslie yelled over his ranting.

"There's nothing left to save!" he rasped.

Somehow over all the noise Leslie heard the doorbell ring and, without excusing herself, she threw up her hands and ran to the door.

Scott stood there, a perplexed look on his face. "What's all the yelling about?" he asked, taking her shoulders protectively and peering around her.

"It's my father," she said, the sight of Scott and his gentle touch calming her exasperation. "I've been trying to reason with him about my mother, but he's so stubborn. And mom left this afternoon to keep from having to confront him." Suddenly she remembered the Chinese food. "Thank you for lunch. Maggie and I loved it." Arching a brow, she whispered, "We'll discuss those fortune-cookie messages later. Now come help me with my dad."

Before he could protest, Leslie was pulling Scott into her kitchen, where Sam stood with the same red-faced, short-fused expression she had left him with. "Dad, I want you to meet Scott Jenkins. Scott, this is my father, Sam Torrence."

"Mr. Torrence," Scott greeted, shaking hands. "I've heard a lot about you."

"That's interesting," Sam said, glaring at Leslie and pulling his hand away from Scott's firm grasp, "since I've heard nothing about you."

"I haven't seen you in a few days," Leslie reminded her father.

"That's right," Sam cut in, shifting his gaze back to Scott. "The last time I saw my daughter she was half-dressed on her way to a date that didn't start until after ten o'clock at night. Was that with you?"

"No, dad," Leslie cut in. "The last time you saw me was when you stormed in here with that first postcard."

Scott suppressed his amusement, but Leslie caught the dimple cracking his cheek. "I don't recall her being half-dressed, and I'm sure I would have remembered. But we *have* had a date that began after ten. You see, I work at night, and I can't get away until then."

"What kind of job doesn't end until ten o'clock? You aren't another doctor, are you?" her father snapped.

"Scott owns some businesses and he has to put in long hours," Leslie said, desperate to shift the direction of the conversation. The last thing she needed was for her father to learn that Scott was Nick Nemoy. Surely he had the sense not to tell him, she thought. "Can I get you some lemonade, Scott?"

Scott nodded his head, but his eyes remained on Sam. In a pleasant voice that in no way lessened the sting of his words, he said, "Leslie tells me you've recently lost a wife."

Sam's eyes shot to Leslie, and she caught her breath. "I can't believe you'd spread gossip about your own parents," he bit out, his face turning a darker crimson.

"Don't blame her," Scott defended. "She only told me because she felt I might be a little responsible."

"Scott!" Leslie warned, stepping close enough to grab his hand in an effort to silence him. He only squeezed it, stopping just before evoking pain, and calmly smiled at her father.

"Responsible how?" her father asked.

"Dad, it was nothing..." But the tighter squeeze of her hand again silenced her words.

"She felt that something I'd said on my radio show had caused your wife to leave."

Sam's icy green eyes shifted from Scott to Leslie, then back to Scott. His bewildered frown faded slowly and turned to uncertain anger. "What did you say your name is?"

"Scott Jenkins!" Leslie blurted, before getting another punishing squeeze of the hand.

"That's my real name," Scott amended, as if he had no idea the revelation would produce more than a nod of the head. "But I have another name I use on the show."

"Oh, no!" Leslie moaned, closing her eyes.

"You may have heard of me," he said. "The notorious Nick Nemoy?"

Leslie couldn't bear to see the look on her father's face, so she jerked her hand free of Scott's and covered her face.

Sam stood up slowly, his eyes taking aim.

"Why you high-and-mighty son of a..."

Leslie looked up in time to see her father rearing a fist to knock through Scott's face. Jumping between them, she pleaded, "Dad, stop it! Scott, go sit over there until I get him calmed down. Go!"

Obediently, Scott retreated and sank into the deep sofa cushions.

"How could you date a man like that?" her father shouted. "How could you do this to me? My own daughter!"

"Dad, I went to see him to tell him just what you want to tell him right now."

"She did," Scott threw in. "She even slugged me, too, if that makes you feel any better."

Her father gaped at him, amazed at his gall.

"But he's not like Nick Nemoy in real life," Leslie said quickly. "Or, he wasn't. Or, I didn't think he was until I saw his performance just now." Her green eyes blazed at Scott, sitting so innocently on the sofa, his calm only adding fuel to the fire building within her.

When Sam was no longer threatening to attack, Scott stood back up. "Look, Mr. Torrence. The way I figure it, if it was my fault, you should thank me. I did you a favor. After all, what kind of woman would walk out on a man after thirty years of marriage?"

"She didn't walk out on me," her father objected loudly.

Scott shrugged. "She filed for separation, didn't she?"

"To make a point," Sam shouted. "I did her wrong. I've been neglecting her and putting everyone else before her."

"Doesn't sound like she needed much attention to me," Scott suggested. "Seems like a woman who takes off on a vacation alone knows exactly how to take care of herself."

"But sometimes a woman needs more!" Sam spluttered. "And I don't need any arrogant radio guy telling me or my wife what state my marriage is in!"

Again Scott shrugged. "I'm just going by the facts. You're here and she's off somewhere all alone."

"Not for long, she's not," Sam raged, turning to Leslie. "I'm going to find her tonight and straighten this mess out, and nobody is going to stop me!" He stormed through the door and slammed it behind him.

Leslie watched through the window, dumbfounded, as her father screeched his car down her driveway, barely avoiding hitting Scott's car, and rocketed off down the street.

Torn between relief that her father had made the right choice, though she wasn't sure how it had happened, and fury at Scott for his obnoxious behavior, she spun around to face him, her eyes blazing like torches.

Scott was grinning from ear to ear. "Well, it worked, didn't it?"

"What worked?" she asked, incredulous.

"Nothing like a little psychology. I just threw his own stand in his face, and he saw how absurd it was."

Leslie gaped at him, unable to comprehend any of what had just happened.

"Man, that wore me out, though." Scott sighed and sat back down. "Almost got beaten to a pulp if you hadn't stepped in. Can I have that lemonade now?"

Leslie leaned toward him, her eyes the size of quarters. "Lemonade? Lemonade? Are you out of your mind? Most men are on their best behavior when they meet the father of the woman they're involved with. You just made an ass of yourself in front of mine and arranged it so that he'll never forgive me for seeing you, and you want lemonade?"

Scott stood up, holding his hands out to calm her. "Les, I swear I'll take care of smoothing things out later. I just thought it was more important to you right now to get your parents back together. And you have to admit it worked."

Leslie's hands went to her temples where a dull throbbing had begun. Scott stepped closer and rested his hands on her shoulders. "I never would have done anything like that just to be obnoxious. I wouldn't hurt you or your father for the world. But you said yourself he was stubborn. Nothing you had tried made him want to work things out. My methods might seem a little odd to you, but they usually get results."

She stepped back out of his grasp. "In other words, the end justifies the means?"

"Something like that. When your parents get back together, he won't even remember all this."

"Are you crazy?" she retorted at her highest volume. "Do you think he'll trot back in here and thank you?"

Scott's mouth quirked upward, and he laughed slightly. "Well, maybe not thank me..."

"Oh, I hate it when you find something funny in everything! Sometimes I just want to slap that smile off your face!"

Only then did Scott realize the gravity of the situation. "Les, you aren't going to hold all this against me, are you?"

Leslie turned away from him, hugging herself around her waist. "That's why I didn't want to go to the station with you. I don't like you when you're Nick Nemoy. I don't like you when you hurt people. Call me too good, and make snide remarks about my ivory tower if you want to, but the fact is that it's *your* attitude that's messed up, not mine!"

Strong hands with the slightest hint of a tremor slid around her waist. "Les, don't do this. Please."

She shoved his hands away and turned toward him, keeping distance between them. "Don't do what? You're the one who's ruined everything."

"Les, I don't want to lose you over this. It's not that important."

"Not important? How can you say that? It's everything!" She raised her hands, fingers spread, and shook her head. "Stephen was right. I don't even know you. All I know of you is what I've wanted to see—Scott Jenkins! But what am I going to do with

the other side of you? I can't stand Nick Nemoy!''
Tears welled and spilled over her lashes, and she batted them away.

Scott reached out to dry her face. "Don't cry," he
whispered.

She slapped his hand away. "Why not? Why
shouldn't I cry? You made me fall in love with you,
Scott. You said in that stupid fortune cookie that
you'd be there to catch me. 'What's the worst that
could happen?' you asked. *This* is the worst that could
happen! I could fall in love with one-half of you and
detest the other half. I could come crashing down to
earth like I just did! And who was there to catch me?
Nick Nemoy? What a joke!''

"I love you, Les," Scott said softly, no longer trying
to narrow the distance between them. "I'm not two
people. I'm one. The man you saw with your father
was Scott Jenkins. I don't turn into Nick Nemoy when
the moon is full. He's there all the time. You fell in
love with *me*. Why is it so hard to accept who I am?''

"Because I want you to be someone else." The admission shocked her, enlightened her, winded her. The
words had been said, and she knew she could never
erase them. When he reached for her again, she did
not back away.

"Don't, Les," he pleaded, lowering his forehead to
rest on her hair. "We were just getting started. Don't
do this to us."

She swallowed hard, but the suffocating lump of
emotion remained in her throat. "I guess I wanted a

fairy tale," she cried into his shirt. "It's just a little hard to come by."

His arms slid around her, and his hand pressed her head against his chest. "I tried to be your champion. As much as a man like me could. I tried to be that fairy-tale knight you've been saving yourself for."

"I know," she whispered. "I just didn't want to see that you're the dragon, too. You'd better go."

"Les," he pressed. "What are you afraid of? I swear I'm not going to hurt you."

"Maybe it's just a matter of time."

"And maybe California will be washed into the Pacific next week, and maybe there'll be a nuclear war tomorrow, and maybe someday you'll wake up and find that somewhere along the road you took a gamble and lost. It's all just a matter of time, right? So why try?" His Nick Nemoy tone was pushing out the Scott Jenkins gentleness, and Leslie felt the muscles knotting in her stomach. But then his voice lowered, and his hands brushed through her hair. "And maybe I'm the one who's in for heartbreak. Maybe it was a stupid idea letting myself get tangled up with a woman who's too good for me." Dropping his hands, he gave a ragged sigh and pulled away from her, his face tight, solemn. "I'll go now, Les, but I won't be back. It'll have to be you who makes the next move."

"Goodbye, Scott," she choked out, opening the door.

Without a word he stalked through it, into the golden hues of sundown that had seen them so close just two days before.

CHAPTER NINE

TWO DAYS LATER, eyes bloodshot and nerves frazzled, Leslie sat at her desk with the telephone propped between ear and shoulder, holding to speak to the IRS about a problem with one of her clients. Absently, numbly, she was drawing in the margin of her notepad—a man in a coat of armor, riding a decrepit black mule. Angry at the unconscious doodling, she scratched it out in heavy black lines, breaking the pencil point. Since she had ended her relationship with Scott Monday night, the hours had been a blur of purely mechanical functioning, as Leslie buried her thoughts in work day and night, trying not to feel the pain of loss tearing at her insides.

Was she plagued, she asked herself, simply because it was the first time since she'd met him that he had actually taken her rejection at face value? Was it bothering her that he hadn't come stampeding her door down, insisting that she was his woman and that the subject was not negotiable? Yes, she admitted, heaving a sigh that caused Maggie to look up from her work with quiet sympathy and an unspoken question in her eyes. Instead of Scott trying to force his way back into her life, it was Stephen, who insisted on helping her through her "phase," promising that he would still be there when she came to her senses. Nothing she said or did convinced him it was over. He was like a man with a mission, who would complete it or die trying.

Impatience finally taking its hold on her, Leslie slammed down the phone. "Drat! It takes three weeks to get a human being on that line!"

Maggie chewed on her pencil, gazing at her. "Wanna talk about it?"

Leslie leaned back in her chair and rubbed her eyes. "What is there to say? They're the IRS. They can treat people like cattle if they want."

"I'm not talking about the IRS," Maggie said with a note of caution. "I'm talking about whatever it is that's had you in mourning the past couple of days."

Leslie wanted to talk, but there seemed to be no words to make things clear. "I'm just nervous because there's so much work to be done. It feels like the walls are closing in on me."

"It's Scott, isn't it?" Maggie probed, as if she hadn't heard her friend.

Defeated, Leslie nodded. Squeezing her eyes shut, she cupped her hands over her face and tried to stop the sudden rush of tears. "I threw him out the other night. It's all over."

Maggie, who had known Leslie since high school, had never seen her fall apart over anything, least of all a man. "Why did you throw him out? What happened? I thought things were going well."

Leslie nodded and tried to regain control of her voice before she went on. "My father was here and Scott insulted him and my mother. He sort of created a common enemy for both my parents—himself—and the next thing I knew, dad was on his way out the door, vowing to find mom and patch things up with her." She stopped and sobbed deeply, then choked out the rest. "I threw him out because of the way he had done it. I told him that I couldn't stand Nick Nemoy, and that I'd never accept him."

"If you can't stand him, then why are you so upset?"

"Because I didn't realize how much I cared about him. I miss him. I haven't even known him that long, and I feel like I've lost some vital part of myself."

Maggie looked down at her hands, then glanced out the window. In a distant voice, she said, "Sounds like love to me."

Leslie took a deep breath and wiped her face. "How can I love someone I'm not even certain I like?"

"Because it's not your choice," Maggie said softly. She leaned forward, her eyes intent on her best friend. "Listen, Leslie, I think you're making a mistake. You're an intelligent person. You wouldn't fall in love with some degenerate. Maybe you're being unfair to him. Maybe in this case your instincts are right."

Leslie stood up and tried to stretch out the fatigue squeezing at her back. "Maybe. It's just that I've always had this picture of what I want in a man. He works hard at a conventional job, and he's dependable and predictable. His life is clean, and no one can find any fault with his methods of doing things. He's respected in the community, and he—"

"Sounds like Stephen," Maggie interrupted.

Leslie sighed. "It does, doesn't it?"

"Fact is, though," Maggie added, "you never really fell in love with Stephen. Or any other of the hundreds of men in this town who fit that description. You fell in love with Scott, someone who made you laugh. Heck, he made me laugh, too. If he weren't so hung up on you, I'd go after him myself."

"That doesn't change the doubts I have," Leslie said.

"Look," Maggie said, "the only way you can get rid of those doubts is to put them on trial. But doubts or no doubts, you're not helping anyone by separating yourself from the only man who has ever made your whole being light up like a Christmas tree. Believe me. I know how rare a feeling like that can be. And losing it might be something you'll regret for the rest of your life. I've been there." A shadow fell over her eyes and she dropped them to the work on her desk.

Leslie knew that Maggie referred to the man she had been engaged to five years earlier. Her reluctance to marry a man who moved from city to city every few weeks, following natural disasters in order to give governmental loans, had ended their relationship, and before she knew it he had left her behind to follow his work.

"And I'll tell you something else," Maggie said, her eyes meeting Leslie's again. "Trying to change a man will only give you gray hair. You've got to decide whether these little flaws you see in him are really worth losing everything over. I'd say they aren't."

Leslie went to the window and peered out, wondering how Scott would react if she went to him and told him she needed him, missed him, loved him. Surely he wouldn't turn her away, she thought. He loved her. But would it be enough to stamp out the doubts? With growing energy and new determination, she turned back to Maggie. "Maggie, I've been working around the clock all week. Would it bother you if I let you hold down the fort for a while so I could go talk to Scott?"

A grin spread across Maggie's face. "Take off," she said. "And good luck. I think this one was meant to be."

Leslie smiled for the first time since Monday and, crossing her fingers, headed for Scott's.

THE SLIDING GLASS DOORS on the side of Scott's house were open when she pulled into the driveway. When she got out of the car, she headed for them instead of the front door. Peeking in between the curtains flapping in the cool April breeze, she caught sight of Scott in his study, his broad shoulders hunched over his desk, his eyes absorbed in the book before him. A ray of sunshine from the doorway lit his hair, spotlighting him in the homey darkness of the room.

She knocked lightly, bringing his attention around to her. "Hi," she said quietly, her face a mixture of apology and caution.

He stood and slid his hands in his pockets. The shirt he wore was unbuttoned, leaving his tanned chest and hard stomach muscles exposed. "I didn't hear you drive up."

"Am I interrupting anything?"

He shrugged. "No. I was just getting some work done." His eyes looked tired, and a shadow of stubble darkened his face. His hair was tousled, adding to the look of fatigue. "Come in."

His quiet manner disturbed her, and she felt awkward and nervous. Stepping inside, she scanned the walls lined with books, and the open ones covering his desktop. Her eyes paused on a table in a corner, where at least a dozen photographs of her were strewn as if he'd just gone through them. "They're good," she said, stepping toward them.

"Not good enough," he answered quietly. "The camera didn't capture everything."

Her eyes went back to his, quiet and waiting— waiting for the move that would tell him what he needed to know.

"I've missed you," she whispered with great effort.

He made no move to touch her. Instead, he let his eyes drift beyond the open doors. "Good."

Suffocating silence followed, and Leslie couldn't tear her eyes from him. What words could she find to mend things?

"How are your parents?" Scott asked.

"I don't know. I haven't heard from either of them."

He nodded. His eyes locked into hers, drawing from her a sudden torrent of emotion. "I'm sorry," she whispered, her eyes welling. "I'll forgive you your flaws if you'll forgive me mine."

His dark eyes softened, and without saying a word, he opened his arms. When she fell into them, she felt a rush of love in every pore. His arms closed tightly around her, his hands molding to her rib cage. His lips made their way down her cheek, finding her mouth, which needed little coaxing to open and welcome him. She leaned into him, straining on tiptoe to reach his level so that she could hold him the way she wanted and love him with the strength of her kiss. He took a step backward, pulling her with him, and leaned against his desk, making himself lower for her. He fit her between his thighs, pressing her against his hard body, his hands exploring her as his tongue played games with hers, drawing her from her protective shell, casting aside her inhibitions.

Combing his fingers through her hair, he pulled back. "I have to be somewhere in fifteen minutes," he whispered. "If I'd known you were coming I'd have canceled."

"I have to go back to work, too," she whispered. "We're swamped. Can you come over tonight before your show?"

"Yes," he whispered, kissing her hair. "I'll be there."

"Scott, I love you," she said.

"I love you, too."

With his arm around her, he walked her to her car and helped her in, then watched her drive away until she was out of sight.

IT WAS SIX-THIRTY when the doorbell rang, and hoping it was Scott, Leslie hurried to answer it. Once again, her mother stood at her door, suitcases in hand. "Mother, what happened?"

"I got bored," Abbie said flatly, coming in. "I was lonely and miserable. I couldn't face another night there alone."

"Didn't dad find you?" Leslie asked, helping her mother with the suitcases and leading her into the living room.

"Find me? No. Was he looking for me?" A spark of hope lit her mother's eyes.

"He sure was. He got in a fight with Scott when he realized he was Nick Nemoy, and before I knew it he was yelling something about how he'd neglected you and how he was going after you to make things right."

Her mother's eyes filled with tears. "Oh, Leslie. Did he really say that?"

Leslie smiled. "Yes, and I told him you were at one of the Holiday Inns. I can't believe he didn't find you."

Abbie's face fell. "I forgot I had told you that. I stayed somewhere else. Oh, no. Now he's going to be tired and angry. He's probably changed his mind by now."

"Don't panic, mom," Leslie said. "He'll be back."

"And I'll be waiting," Abbie said, hurrying to the guest room. "Excuse me. I've got to do something with my hair."

Her mother had scarcely disappeared when the doorbell rang again. Praying it would be her father, Leslie opened it. Stephen greeted her.

"Stephen, you shouldn't be here," she told him as he pushed into the house.

"I told you, Leslie. I'm not giving up on you. I didn't want you to be alone tonight, so I brought my books over here to study."

"Stephen, I don't want you to study here. I have other plans."

Stephen dropped his books on the table and turned back to her. "With Jenkins?"

"Yes," she said.

"So he's squirmed his way back into your life?"

Leslie gritted her teeth. "I went to see him today. He's coming over here before his show, and I don't want you to be here."

"Why not? You never had any qualms about bringing *him* here when you were involved with me."

"Stephen, I don't have to explain this to you. Please go home."

Stephen slammed his fist on the table, propped his foot on a chair and pinched the bridge of his nose. "Leslie, I can't deal with this kind of instability in my life. I need some consistency if I'm going to keep doing well in school."

"Stephen, things couldn't be more stable. We are over. Finished. I'm involved with Scott. How much more consistent could I be?"

"Dammit, Leslie," he said, tears filling his eyes. "I need you. I counted on you. There were other women I could have had. I looked a long time. But you were just right for me. You didn't put a lot of demands on me, you didn't expect too much and you didn't need more than I could give."

"You didn't *give* anything, Stephen," she said, realizing it for the first time. "If I fit into that little mold you had for your wife, it was because I forced myself to. I'm not right for you, Stephen. And you're not right for me. It's over. Even if Scott and I can't make it last, there's nothing left for you and me."

His tears spilled over, and he covered his eyes with a hand. Leslie watched his body shake with sobs, and a sudden wave of sympathy washed over her. She went to him, wrapped her arms around his waist and hugged him. He hung on to her, pulling her closer than she wanted, his wet bristled face bending toward her unwilling one. His embrace was crushing as his lips closed over hers, prying her mouth open, bruising her as if the pressure would bring her back to him. She tried to push him away, but he only clamped her tighter, his teeth grinding painfully into her mouth until she tasted blood.

As Leslie struggled fruitlessly, she heard voices and the closing of a door. The intrusion softened Stephen's hold on her, and at last she broke free.

Scott was standing in the doorway, her mother behind him. His eyes were eloquent with pain and betrayal. Without a word, he walked back to the door and slammed it behind him.

"Scott!" she shouted, running after him, but by the time she had reached the door he was in his car and screeching out of her driveway.

"I'm sorry," her mother said softly. "I let him in without knowing..."

Ignoring her mother, Leslie turned to Stephen. "Get out!" she screamed. "Get out of here and don't ever come back!"

"He's going to hurt you!" Stephen warned, gathering his books. "You're better off without him!"

"I love him!" she shouted, crying into her hands. "Get out of my life!" When he'd gone through the door, she slammed it behind him with all the force and fury she could find within her. "And stay out!" she yelled through the wood, knowing it didn't matter anymore.

Scott was gone, and nothing mattered anymore.

CHAPTER TEN

"LESLIE, YOU'RE BLEEDING!" Abbie wailed when her daughter turned back to her, shaken and devastated.

"Mother, he's gone. He thought..."

Abbie rushed into the kitchen and wet a paper towel, then came running back to Leslie to dab the cut on the inside of her lip. "It's all my fault. I heard a car pull into the driveway and thought it might be your father, so I just answered the door. I didn't know Stephen was here."

Leslie took the wet paper towel and wiped her tears. "Everything's ruined. Scott saw him kissing me, and he probably thinks it was all some cruel joke that I set up. How do I convince him that it wasn't that way at all?"

"You go after him," her mother said. "You get in your car and find him and just tell the truth."

Leslie straightened, took a deep breath, made up her mind. "All right. He'll just have to believe me. I'll just have to convince him."

Rushing out to her car, she got in and took a deep breath. The clock on the dashboard said six forty-five. He wouldn't have gone to the studio yet, she thought. Cranking up her car and pulling out of the driveway, she decided to go to his house. Rehearsing a hundred different ways to tell him she loved him, that there would never be anyone else, she raced through the seemingly endless streets to Scott's.

Pulling into his driveway, she saw that his car was not there and the lights in the house were off. Mumbling an expletive, she backed out of the drive again and headed for the radio station. His car wasn't there, either. After checking out several spots in New Orleans she had heard him mention, she gave up. She would have to go home and wait until his show was over. She would just have to hope she would not be too late.

When she got home, her mother greeted her at the door. "Did you find him?"

"No," Leslie said dismally.

"He came back after you left," Abbie told her hurriedly. "When I opened the door he stormed in and demanded to see you. If Stephen had still been here I think he would have killed him." Her mother's eyes danced with the drama, and Leslie smiled with relief.

"What did he say?"

"He said that he wasn't going to let you go that easily. Said you may be having second thoughts, but he intended to turn you around."

Leslie laughed, throwing her hands up in the air. "Did you tell him I didn't have any second thoughts?"

Abbie shook her head. "All I had time to tell him was that Stephen had forced that kiss on you and that if he'd hung around long enough he would have seen the blood on your mouth to prove it."

"Oh, no, mom. What did he say?"

Abbie took Leslie's shoulders. "He said that no matter what he did he kept letting you down. And then he left, muttering that it was time to end this once and for all."

Leslie's face fell, and fresh tears sprang to her eyes. "Just like that? He gives up just like that?"

Abbie hugged her daughter. "I'm sorry, honey. I tried to stop him, but he flew out of here like a man possessed."

Sinking onto the couch, Leslie stared at the coffee table in front of her. Where did she go from here?

When the doorbell rang, she jumped up to answer it, praying it was Scott. It was her father.

Coming in, he rubbed his hand through his hair. "I'm worried about Abbie," he said. "I looked in every hotel up and down the coast and couldn't find her. Do you think she's done something drastic?"

"Drastic enough," her mother said from the doorway of the foyer. "I came back."

"Abbie!" her father bellowed, staring toward her, then catching himself and stopping. "Where the hell have you been? Has this all been some kind of conspiracy or something?"

Leslie collapsed against the door. "No, dad. She just came home a little while ago. She wanted to see you. Please don't ruin it." Her lip was beginning to swell, and her head throbbed with misery, but her father only had eyes for her mother.

"Me ruin it? I haven't done anything yet. Abbie, you're coming home with me tonight, do you hear? I've had enough of all this. You're driving me crazy!"

"I'm driving you crazy? Senile is more the word!"

"Senile? You call me senile? That's better than just plain eccentric! Running off to who knows where whenever the going gets rough! Get your things. You're coming home with me!"

"I am not going anywhere with you in that mood!" She moved out of the foyer into the office to get farther away from him, and he followed her.

"This is not a mood! This is frustration! I don't know how to deal with you anymore." Reaching for her hand, he gave it a tug. "Now come home with me right now!"

Abbie jerked her hand from his and picked up a staple gun that sat on Leslie's desk. Aiming it at her husband, she backed away. "Come near me again and I'll shoot!"

"You wouldn't dare," Sam said, eyes ablaze.

"Just try me," Abbie riposted, "and you'll have a staple right between the eyes."

The absurdity of the situation hit Sam first, and he leaned his hands on the desk, dropped his head and smiled. A slow current of laughter began to shake his shoulders. When he stood up and tried to cover his face, his amusement became audible. The laughter was contagious, and soon Abbie smiled too, dropped the staple gun and took part.

"Aha!" Sam shouted, jumping around the table and grabbing her. "She's unarmed, Leslie! I've got her!"

Still laughing, Abbie collapsed against his shoulder, and his embrace became tender. "I love you, you crazy woman," he said softly. "Come home with me and I swear you'll see a change. Besides, we have to pack for our cruise. I've rescheduled it. We leave this weekend."

"No," Abbie wailed. "No cruises. Please!"

Leslie smiled as her father got her mother's suitcases, the bickering never stopping. "It was your idea. I thought you'd always wanted to take a cruise."

"The thought makes me sick already. Please. Can't we just stay home for a while?"

"We'll see. I've got some travel brochures at home. Maybe you'll change your mind. It'll all be different with me there," he said with calm self-assurance as he opened the front door.

Suddenly remembering Leslie's plight, Abbie turned to her daughter. "Oh, honey, I forgot about you. Sam, we can't leave her. She's going through a dilemma."

"I can take care of it, mom," Leslie promised. "You two go home."

"Is it that Nemoy character?" Sam asked bluntly.

Leslie nodded. "Sorry, dad, but I'm in love with him."

A restrained smile touched Sam's mouth. He sighed heavily. "Well, I'll tell you one thing about him. He's smarter than I used to give him credit for. Knew how to handle me, didn't he?" Shaking his head, he laughed. "Yessir, I guess you could do a lot worse."

Leslie felt half her burden drain from her shoulders, and suddenly it seemed that her father's blessing brought a whole new light to things. If her father could change his mind, maybe she could change Scott's. Maybe it wasn't too late.

"Then again, you could do a lot better," he said with the beginnings of a frown.

"Oh, hush," Abbie teased. "You haven't met him as Scott Jenkins yet. He'll charm your socks off! Go after him, Leslie," she said, turning to her daughter. "There's still time."

"I will," she said, walking out to the car with her parents. Smiling, she watched as her father loaded the car with her mother's luggage, then scooted in next to her, reaching for her hand and setting it on his knee.

Leslie watched as they drove off, her heart happy for them, but at the same time heavy with the need to see Scott. She lifted her head and gazed at the sky, full and dark and overcast with clouds that forewarned of a storm. It had been that way the first night she'd met Scott, she remembered. The smell of rain had been prominent in the air, and the breeze had been sprinkled with mist. The sky had been dark except for the occasional quiet flash of lightning miles away. He had drawn her under his spell that night, and when she'd learned he was Nick Nemoy, nothing had really changed. She had still been his captive, despite the two sides to the man that seemed to contradict each other. The knight and the dragon, feuding with each other....

Funny how things changed. For in her mind and heart, the knight wasn't quite perfect and the dragon didn't seem as big, nor as contemptible, as he had before. She loved them both. Scott Jenkins and Nick Nemoy would forever have to battle for her love.

It was after eight when Leslie had pulled herself together enough to go after him again. His show started and she knew she couldn't see him until it was over, but she was unwilling to sit in one place and wait.

So she got into her car and drove the back streets of New Orleans, listening to Scott at work.

The dialogue on Nick's show had to do with the teachers' strike. A taxpayer was complaining about their grievances. "I have to say I agree with you," the host said, surprising Leslie into listening more closely. "I mean, how much can the taxpayers be expected to pay for education? Why should you pay higher taxes so somebody else's kid can learn to read?"

"I'm not saying I mind paying the taxes," the caller said defensively. "It's not that at all. I just don't think it's worth what they're asking.".

"I know what you mean," Nick Nemoy said. "I've had it with all this rhetoric about the textbooks being outdated. Columbus still discovered America in 1492, the Civil War still ended in 1865. And what's been happening in Lebanon and on the moon this century has been overrated, anyway. Right, fella?"

"Not exactly. I think probably we could do better with the textbooks—"

"But then you'd have to have teachers with something between their ears to teach from the new textbooks. Let's face it. All we're really talking about is glorified baby-sitters with three-month vacations. Everyone knows the real source of education these days is television." *Click.* "This is Nick Nemoy. Go ahead."

"I'm a teacher!" someone said hotly. "And I resent that last comment. You try taking a six-year-old child and letting television teach him to read!"

"Big deal. It's like talking. Everyone does it sooner or later." *Click.* "Hello, you're on the air."

Leslie drove and listened incredulously as she heard the way Scott inspired dialogue between the callers, how he drew both sides of the story from them and filled in the gaps of information that were left out, how he inserted figures and statistics in a negative way, as if arguing against the teachers, when she realized his absurd stand would sway listeners in the teachers' favor.

Before the show was over, she realized how carefully he had researched the teachers' predicament and the financial situation of the state. She saw that he had studied every exchange of dialogue in the legislature about the problem, and knew which politicians were on the side of the teachers and which were not.

And because she had listened to his show, she knew now, too. Scott Jenkins believed in his show because it made a positive contribution to society. And two hundred conformists couldn't have done a better job than that one man who did things his own way. Her heaviness lifted as she drove, giving her the strange ecstatic feeling that things would be all right.

It was nine forty-five when she decided to go to the station and wait for him, as she had done that night that seemed so long ago. She would simply try to take up from there; start over, if possible, with only the love that had grown from instinct and need, without her prejudices against his stage name and profession.

The station lobby was empty, as it had been the first night she'd marched in there ready to take on the man who had split up her parents' marriage. She laughed under her breath at the memory, realizing how effective his methods had been for her parents. She had expected him to look like W.C. Fields, she remembered. Perhaps if her mind had been more open, she would have known at the beginning that Nick Nemoy was the handsome charming blond stranger who had greeted her.

She went to the speaker on the wall and turned the switch so that she could hear the show. Scott was in some rather heated dialogue with a caller about the conviction of a cult leader for tax fraud.

"It's people like you I worry about," he clipped in his radio voice. "People with peanut butter for brains, just waiting for someone to reach in and spread it around to the corners."

Leslie burst out laughing, then slapped her hand over her mouth. She wanted to rush down the hall and into his studio and throw her arms around him. But she feared that such an act would throw him off balance and he'd lose his momentum. Her eyes caught sight of the phone on the empty reception desk, and she smiled mischievously.

His number was written beside one of the buttons on the phone, so she picked up the receiver and dialed it. Her heart thumped loudly as the phone rang several times, unanswered. Nick was finishing giving his graphic opinion of the current caller's intelligence.

Her heart leaped when she heard the famous *click* on the radio. In her ear, the notorious talk-show host answered, "This is Nick Nemoy, go ahead."

"Nick Nemoy," Leslie said into the phone, using her most seductive voice, "I have a serious problem, and I need advice."

"And what might that problem be?" he asked quickly, as if his finger were on the button, ready to cut her off.

"I've been living in an ivory tower. I'm ready to escape, but I can't do it alone."

A few seconds of silence followed, and Leslie tried to picture him as he realized whom he was speaking to. "It's easy," he said a little more slowly than usual. "Ivory towers are full of windows. All you have to do is jump."

"What if there's no one there to catch me?" she asked softly.

"You know someone will be there," he answered, slipping out of his Nick Nemoy voice into the velvety cadence of Scott Jenkins. "It's just a matter of choice. A knight in tarnished armor can help a damsel in distress as well as the next guy. The trick is knowing she's in distress. Sometimes he doesn't know if she wants to be caught."

"How can I let him know?" she asked, tears of relief coming to her eyes.

A few more seconds passed, and Leslie smiled as Nick was speechless for the first time since she'd known him. "Maybe he's a bit of a schmuck," he said finally. "Maybe you'll have to marry him to convince him."

Leslie caught her breath. "Marry him?" She cleared her throat and laughing softly said, "I think I need that advice in person."

"Believe me, you'll get it," he rumbled for all to hear.

Biting her lip, she hung up, listening to the speaker on the wall as she heard Scott clear his throat, falter, then pick up. "Rack your brains to figure that one out," he told his audience with a laugh. "I have to go now. My steed grows restless. This is Nick Nemoy, signing off."

Leslie took a deep breath as Scott's theme music took over. Standing up and crossing to the doorway he'd soon be coming through, she leaned against the wall so that he wouldn't see her until he was in the room with her.

Her heart stopped as she heard his footsteps coming hurriedly along the hall, but it leaped to life when he came through the doorway, flying past her.

"Scott."

He swung around and caught his breath at the sight of her. "Les."

His eyes drank her in. With almost the width of the room still between them, she saw his throat move as he swallowed. "You called me from here?"

Nodding her head, she rushed into his arms, warm and strong and everything she had hoped they'd be. "I thought I'd lost you," she whispered tearfully. "I thought you had given up on us after you saw Stephen..."

At the mention of his name, Scott's hands closed gently around her face and he eased her away from him. "Are you okay? Did he hurt you?"

"Yes, I'm fine. It's just my lip," she answered, bewildered.

Hugging her tightly against him again, he buried his face in her hair. "God, I'm such a jerk. How could I have left you there with him? I thought you had gone back to him. I didn't know he was forcing you...."

"It's all right," she said in a soothing voice. "It's all over now. I don't think he'll be back."

Scott looked at her, his dark eyes blazing with anger. "You better know he won't be back. I went after him when your mother told me what he did to you."

"You didn't hurt him, did you?"

Scott grinned at the memory, and he leaned back on the empty desk. "Let's just say that I breathed a little fire in his face. Didn't have to do anything else. He was so scared he would have sworn to anything. He won't bother you again."

Touching his face with fingers that trembled from a love so great that her body had not got used to dealing with it yet, she brought her sparkling green eyes to his. "I love you, Scott."

"I love you, too," he whispered, kissing her gently to keep from hurting her lip. "You remember when I said I had to be somewhere today when you came over?" he asked, pulling back from her and reaching in his shirt pocket. "I had to go get this." He pulled out a tiny box and closed his hand over it. "I'd made the appointment before our fight Monday night, and I couldn't make myself cancel it. When you came over today, I decided to keep it." He opened the brown velvet box, revealing an enormous glowing emerald on a gold band.

"Like your eyes," he whispered. "I would have got you a diamond, but you know how I hate to be like everybody else."

Leslie's eyes welled with fresh tears at the beauty of the stone and the love that had gone behind it. She groped for words, but found none.

"Just say yes," he whispered, taking the ring out and putting in on her left hand. "Just say you'll marry me."

"Of course I'll marry you," she answered in a hoarse voice, between breaths. "If you can tolerate my ivory tower."

He smiled, his voice a murmur against her throat. "Absolutely," he said, "if you can tolerate my dragons."

"Absolutely," she echoed. "After all, I'm getting such a great guy."

Scott pulled her out of the station into the night air, an enormous grin lighting his face. "Finally, she believes me," he said, looking heavenward.

In the distance, a lightning bolt flashed, and Scott pulled her into his arms. "Looks like there's going to be another storm tonight," he whispered, just before his lips closed over hers, "but this one's going to last a long, long time."

Coming Next Month in Harlequin Romances!

2749   A MATTER OF MARNIE   Rosemary Badger
Convincing an Australian construction tycoon that his
grandmother has been neglected is a formidable task. Living with
him in order to care for the woman is an even greater challenge.

2750   THE PERFECT CHOICE   Melissa Forsythe
A voice student in Vienna seldom turns men's heads. So when a
handsome stranger woos her, she's in too deep by the time she
discovers his motive for choosing her over her beautiful friend.

2751   SAFE HARBOUR   Rosalie Henaghan
This trustworthy secretary weathers her boss's changeable moods
until his woman friend predicts an end to Anna's working days—
and sets out to make her prophecy come true.

2752   NEVER THE TIME AND THE PLACE   Betty Neels
The consulting surgeon at a London hospital disturbs his ward sister's
natural serenity. She's having enough trouble coping with a broken
engagement without having to put up with his arrogance.

2753   A WILL TO LOVE   Edwina Shore
That the family's Queensland homestead should be sold is
unthinkable. But the only way to save it—according to her
grandfather's will—is to marry the same man who rejected her
four years ago.

2754   HE WAS THE STRANGER   Sheila Strutt
The manager of Milk River Ranch knew that a male relative would
inherit her uncle's spread. But why did the beneficiary have to be a
writer who would either sell out or take over completely?

Can you keep a secret?

You can keep this one plus 4 free novels
